Printed in the United States of America

First Printing, 2015

This is a work of fiction. Names, characters, businesses, places, events and incidents are either the products of the author's imagination or used in a fictitious manner. Any resemblance to actual persons, living or dead, or actual events is purely coincidental.

Matthew Davis

rockandhillstudio@gmail.com

ISBN-13: 9781517558086

ISBN-10: 1517558085

Rock and Hill Studio Production

Cover and Book Design by Matt Davis

Editing by Walt Shuler

Interior Art by Will Kirkby

www.chamonkee.tumblr.com

First Edition

"When the going gets weird, the weird turn pro."

\- Hunter S. Thompson

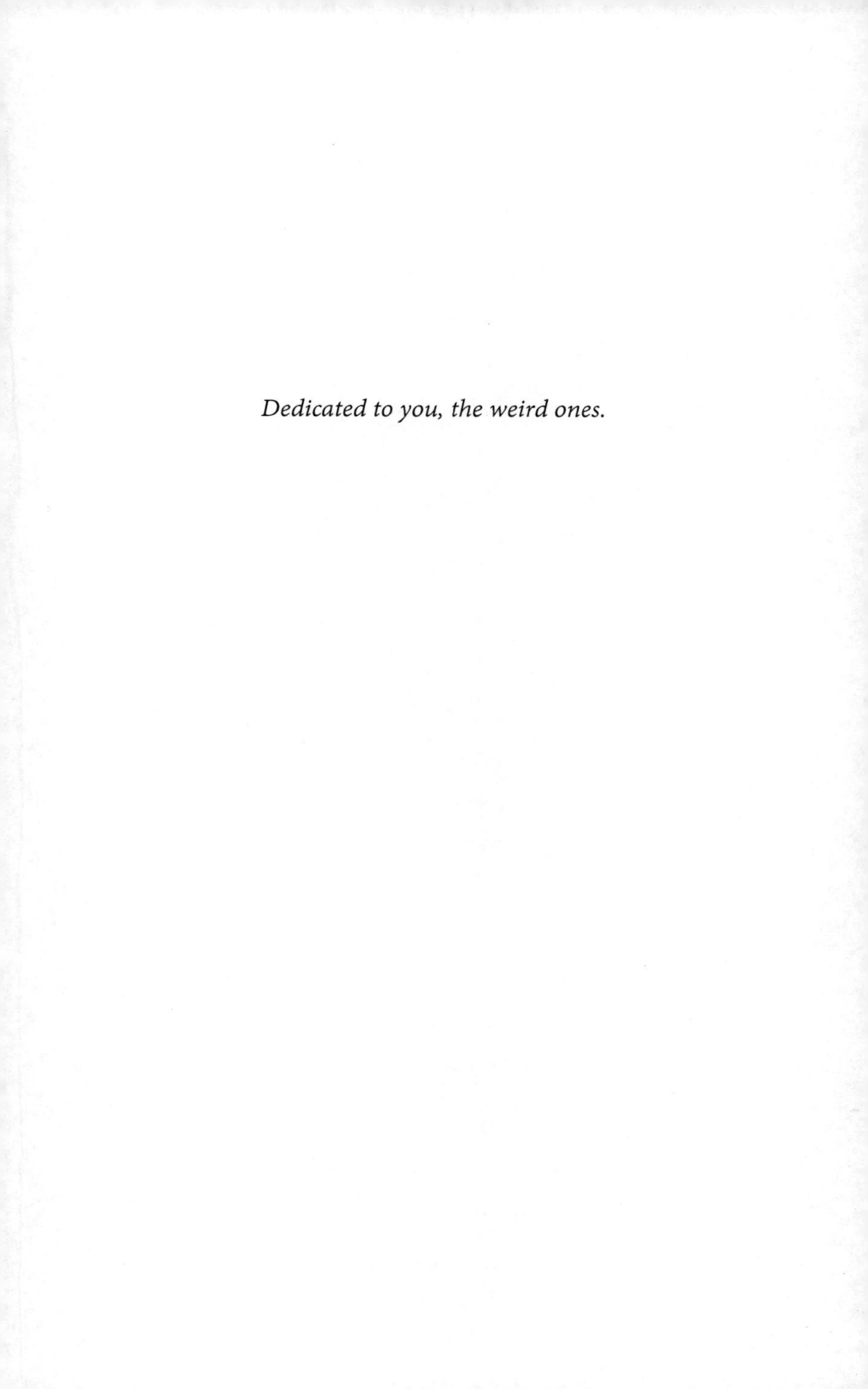

Dedicated to you, the weird ones.

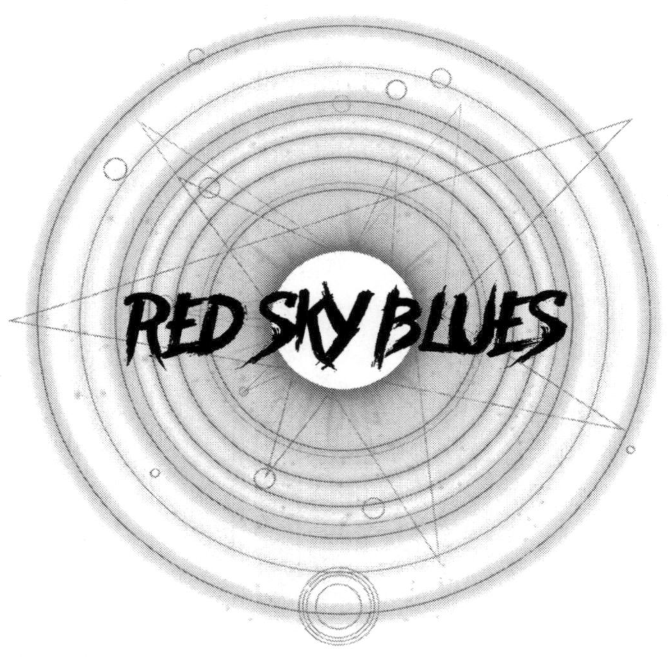
RED SKY BLUES

1

It's worth noting that shifting through the spectrum isn't the easiest thing in the world to describe.

There are layers to reality, usually invisible, co-existing parallel to each other. Some talented, magical people come into the world born with the knack for looking through those layers. They can witness the full spectrum of reality.

None of it makes sense, not in a way that's neat and proper to the human mind. Years ago, people who saw the true nature of the world became madmen and prophets, but in recent years learned to keep their damn mouths shut because it sounds fucking crazy even thinking about it. The grand, terrifying face behind the mask the world wears. Slipping along the spectrum begins with the taste of blood in the back of my throat and a sensation like tiny, blunt-toothed worms gnawing their way into the backs of my eyeballs. That's when the mask peels back, when it begins to get interesting, and the Other Side shows itself.

It's also painful, as the truth usually is.

The whole time there's the feeling of a slender blade like a scalpel working its way into the folds of my brain, and it never stops hurting. It hurts every time, and has my entire life since awakening to it, but I like to think I've grown accustomed to the pain. It's a fair enough trade. A solid bargain for seeing the strange side of life that exists right in front of us. Invisible worlds within reach if only people knew how to see.

The old Asian guy for instance, sitting by himself near the windows near the front of the café, enjoying the sun. To anyone else, he looked like a happy, wizened old man nursing a cup of coffee and working at a crossword puzzle in the local paper. But as my gaze passed over him, I got that familiar tingle in my skull that let me know there was something Other about him. I slid my vision along the spectrum, reality shifted and blurred, and the old timer stood out like a bizarre sore thumb. The proportions and framework, the mold was all still close enough to humanoid. Instead of wrinkled brown skin, he had a black carapace that shimmered like oil, and humongous compound eyes like scarlet gemstones took up the bulk of his head. Between those eyes sprouted a delicate, snake-like proboscis and he had two extra arms that ended in vicious talons folded up against his torso.

He didn't look at me, content to go about his façade and enjoy his coffee and crossword, so I dropped back along the spectrum and went about my business. Most of the time the Others, those who came from beyond our reality, tended to let humanity go about with its delusion of believing it ruled the world. And I was happy enough to perpetuate the lie.

I made it to the counter and rifled through my pockets for change, my craving for caffeine having become unbearable on the long walk into town. I'd had no good reason to leave home until Devlin called wanting a meeting, which of course he insisted be at a trendy coffee shop at a ridiculous hour when even the sun was being lazy about getting on with the day.

"Yeah, hi. Can I get a...coffee? You do have coffee, right? The regular kind?" I asked while scanning the menu hanging behind the counter, and looked down to see the barista giving me a glacial look.

"Of course we have coffee," the guy said after an angst-laden sigh. "Tall, grande, or venti?"

I blinked at him. "What? Is that, is that some kind of code?" I looked back over my shoulder for a second and then turned back and dumped my change on the countertop. "Can I just get a small?"

I heard his teeth grind as he went and filled a small paper cup with coffee from a chrome dispenser behind him, putting a lid on it before handing it to me.

I gave him a thumbs up and what I hoped was a winning smile before spinning on my heels and walking to a secluded table in the far corner of the shop away from the crowd to wait for Devlin. I let my bag slip off my shoulder and thud onto the seat next to me, trying not to look completely obvious as I scanned the room and watched the people go about their business.

The crowd was about what one would expect, made up

of hipsters, fogies, bustling business types, and other random members of humanity at large. But what shocked me the most was the sheer number of them. Who knew so many people were up and about at six for-the-love-of-god-o'clock in the morning? It had been so long since I last woke up at such an early hour that I had almost given up believing the early morning existed, thinking instead it to be a distant, disturbing memory of an even more disturbing dream.

I couldn't imagine what Devlin would want that required me to be anywhere so early, but I couldn't shake the feeling that it wouldn't be good. People only arranged meetings at crowded public places when something terrible was going to happen. At least there was coffee--I would take any silver linings I could get. So instead of brooding, I slumped down in my seat and cradled my cup, inhaling the steam and waiting for it to cool down from boiling lava hot to something meant for human consumption.

"Thomas!" The high, clear voice exploded across the room and almost gave me a heart attack. "My dear, dear boy I was afraid you wouldn't show."

Cringing, I turned to look to the door and saw that every

head in the room had done the same thing.

Devlin Desmund, ladies and gentlemen.

Like my friend the bug-man, to everyone else in the room he looked like a kind old gentleman somewhere around a spry, healthy eighty. He could have been somebody's grandpa, complete with thick, gold-wire spectacles, knit sweater vest, and a fringe of cotton white hair slicked down around his head. He shuffled along in battered penny-loafers with actual pennies in them, his gnarled walking stick clicking as he went. He smiled at me as he ambled along, stopping here and there to pat some-one on the shoulder or murmur a greeting. But, like my friend the bug-man, he was much more than he first appeared. No one would ever guess that he was not only one of the single most powerful Others in town, but the reigning monarch of Hanford as well, a benevolent, albeit inhuman ruler from the shadows. I noticed the elderly bug-man slip out as Devlin came in, and gave a peek across the spectrum--which ended up being a dreadful idea. I ended up catching a glimpse of Devlin's true form, which snapped me back to normal like a crowbar between the eyes and left me with a metallic taste in my mouth and a ringing in my ears. Flashes of manifold ephemeral limbs and sun-bright globes orbiting a shape that defied geometry burned themselves onto my retinas and I almost dropped my coffee into my lap.

"Thomas, you look as if you've had a fright, whatever is the matter?" Devlin asked after finally making his way to the table and sat down, laying his walking stick across his knees.

"I think I might have burned out some brain cells, but I wasn't using them anyways, thanks."

I set my coffee down with shaking hands and looked across at him. He was watching me, looking me over with too bright eyes that were no human shade of blue, smiling a knowing smile like there was a hilarious joke and I had missed the punchline. Or maybe I was the punchline. He drummed his fingers on his cane and waited for me to say something.

"What have you gone and dragged me out of bed for Devlin?" I relented and asked finally. "Your messenger made it sound like it was the end of the world."

"Oh, Thomas, it can wait. How are you? It's been ages. All better after that tussle with those, oh what did they call themselves? The Broken Circle or some nonsense?" He let out a bit of a laugh. “I dare say you do look a bit ragged I’m afraid.”

I cringed.

The Broken Circle. Flashing back to that encounter sent a cold shiver through me and brought back unwelcome memories of slime and crawling things with more legs than anything had a right to have. I cleared my throat and turned away from Devlin, catching a glimpse of myself in the nearby window as I did so. He must have decided to be polite when he said ragged because I looked like a deranged vagrant and was kind of surprised no one had called the police.

I wore a much-battered Army issue coat that was a couple sizes too large for me, and wore a hooded sweater beneath that which combined made me look somewhat on the lumpy side, and I hadn’t cut my hair or beard since it had all managed to grow back--acidic ichor, what were you going to do, right? My hair looked like a rat had recently nested in it, snarled and tangled in a half dozen directions and the coarse black beard that hung from my face was in a similar state of disarray. There were dark circles around my eyes that looked like bruises, or a particularly bad makeup job. And maybe it was something about the light and the reflection in the glass, or the lack of proper nutrition, but I looked like a malnourished goblin. I might have become something of a recluse after my encounter with the Broken Circle. Come to think of it, this was my first real foray beyond my home since that incident that didn't involve raiding the local ninety-nine cent store for supplies. I might have to do some grooming after Devlin told me what was going on, make an attempt at looking human if I was going to continue being out in public.

"I'm fine, and your precious barony is no longer infested by dimension devouring cockroach worshippers." I was aiming for smug but it might have come out indignant. I shrugged. "You're welcome."

"My subjects and I thank you, Thomas; we are in your debt," Devlin said.

"You can thank me with a check," I said over the rim of my cup. "Or cash."

"In due time, of course. Humans and your money--all so sad and transient." Devlin's friendly, paternal smile faded as he spoke. He looked at me with lambent eyes, and for an uncomfortable moment the gravity in the room ratcheted up, "I digress, forgive me. Since pleasantries are over with, might we move on to business?"

"Yes, please."

"I assume you know of the Libro Nihil?"

I rolled the words around in my head and they set off a few alarms, so I dove deeper, sorting through the trove of lore I kept locked deep within my grey matter. My business was information; secrets were my stock and trade, and over the years, I'd accumulated an awful lot to sort through. It took a few seconds of stumbling around the labyrinthine corridors of my memory palace but at last I got to what I was after.

"A book penned and enchanted during the First Crusade by an insane ascetic mage of an unknown order, reputed to give the wielder the means to contact, summon, and compel entities from the Void and Beyond," I recited the information at last, staring into my coffee as I spoke, turning over other bits of fact and memory. "It's been sought after for centuries and mentioned in quite a few horrific passages of occult history. Also, I'm pretty sure it's a faery tale."

I looked up at Devlin and something of his playful smile

had returned, the lights dancing in his eyes.

"And why do you say that?" he asked, inclining his head.

I shrugged and swirled my cup around. "Because for all that it has been spoken of over the centuries, I've never heard of anyone actually having the damn thing, except dead men of which there's also conveniently no legitimate record. Even the author's a total unknown. It's all speculation, second and third-hand encounters" I took a drink of my coffee, my throat had gone dry. It had been a while since I'd spoken to a real person. "It's the god damn bogeyman of evil books."

"Impressive as usual, my boy. Impressive. But what if I were to tell you a secret?" He leaned across the table to stage whisper, "What if I told you it was not a faery tale?"

I sat a moment and let his words sink in. Of course it could be true, the Libro could exist and have been well hidden for a long time, passing from owner to owner and leaving a trail of death and madness in its wake. Stranger things had happened with shocking regularity throughout the course of history. But if it were out there in the world and could do all the terrible things it could do then why wasn't there a higher frequency of invasions from sanity bending gods of nihilism?

"I would be damn curious where you got your info," I said at last.

"My source prefers to remain anonymous for the time being, but I was hoping to acquire your services. You've been in the dark too long, Thomas. Come back into the light and help me." Devlin damn near sounded sincere, almost concerned, which was kind of weird.

The fact that he would pay was tempting enough by itself, money was a non-object to Devlin and he had always paid me well in the past for my services or information. He had been, in many ways, my primary source of income. I liked money an awful lot; you could do all kinds of neat things with it like buy real food that didn't come in tin cans and pay looming electric bills. Over the last couple months, my savings had dwindled down to a pittance subsidized by whatever I could find between the couch cushions.

"Tell it to me straight, then. What is it you want from me, Devlin?" I asked and did my level best to not sound too eager.

"I want you to find the book, of course. I have been recently told it has come to the valley, to Hanford no less," Devlin said, pointing a finger at the tabletop for emphasis. "It is of the utmost importance that the Libro Nihil not fall into the wrong hands, Thomas. I cannot stress that enough. We must secure it and deal with it in a proper fashion. There are too many Others that call this town sanctuary that would be all too eager to abuse something like that book to malicious ends."

He was right, of course, but I was suspicious of Devlin's motives. If the Libro Nihil were capable of even a fraction of the atrocities against reality attributed to it and someone figured out how to use it then that would spell bad business for everyone. The Broken Circle trying to spread corrosive spiritual pollution through the city's water supply was one thing, but what we were talking about was several magnitudes of terrible beyond that.

"All right, I'm in," I said and raised a hand before Devlin could say something. "But I want my full rate for the job, and it'll take me some time to get myself sorted and find out what I can about the book, especially if you're not interested in sharing your contact."

"Excellent, most excellent. You can reach me through the

usual channels should there be anything you need. And please, do be careful." With that Devlin rose, patting me on the shoulder as he passed by, and made his way out of the coffee shop, cane clicking along as he went.

Something had my hackles up about the situation. Devlin had any number of sources on the Other Side that he could command to hunt down the book without having to pay a single cent. And speaking of sources, who was the mysterious informant that told him of the Libro Nihil to begin with? That was a slimy question and one worth looking into. Part of me hoped that it was all a farce, bad info and superstition and I would end up pounding the streets only to tell Devlin that it was a bad hoax.

"Yeah, right," I muttered.

Things around town were about to get even weirder than usual; I could feel it. Small towns like Hanford were magnets for supernatural strangeness, isolated pockets of humanity where the barriers between the layers of reality broke down and let things slip through. Smalltown, USA was a great place to find demons and monsters hiding out in their people-skin masks, up to who the hell knew what. And Hanford was as strange as places came, the whole Valley reeked of the Other Side's weirdness. Keep a low profile and an extra-dimensional energy parasite could fit right in

Enough meandering; if any of it was as serious as it had the potential to be, I needed to get moving. I shouldered the weight of my bag as I stood and got more coffee before I made my way out of the shop, grateful for the free refill policy. I cringed once I got outside. Add sunglasses to the list of things to get when I had money. It had been comfortable and dim when I left my hovel, now the sun was rising into the sky and glaring down on the world with a vengeance, and there were people everywhere; scads of them all going about and rushing off to normal jobs, intent on whatever the business of the day was.

I cut into the alley behind the strip mall the cafe was located in and started the walk back home. My head was swimming with scraps of thoughts, fleeting bits of the conversation with Devlin, half-remembered pieces of arcane trivia, and I was so involved with piecing things together that I didn't notice when my brain started humming. A metallic grating filled my ears and the backs of my eyes began to itch. Something from the Other Side was close, and getting closer fast.

I had enough time to shift through the spectrum before the bug-guy from the coffee shop hurtled through the air and crashed into me, riding me to the ground. Four inhuman arms and every one of them were trying to pound me into the earth. I went down with a grunt, coffee went flying and my bag hit the dirt, spilling its contents everywhere.

"You will not have the book!" the bug-man howled in a whining, metallic voice.

I knew I shouldn't have gotten out of bed today.

2

There went a rib.

That was definitely a rib. I could feel when it popped and gave way, and Bugbrain kept swinging, four arms working in tandem to pulverize me.

My heavy coat and sweater didn't amount to much in the way of armor, and to make matters worse, Bugbrain's snake-like proboscis was whipping about and making a nerve-rattling squeal while an oily fluid oozed from the pronged mouth at the end. The damn thing was whipping about right in front of my face, snapping with tiny, needle teeth.

He was too damn strong, way stronger than I could hope to match. Four fists smashing into you like jackhammers was a lot to deal with, and it was all I could do to try to pull myself into the fetal position and give him a smaller target--and then a drop of viscous saliva from Bugbrain's proboscis fell and landed square on my face with a sizzle and a pop.

"Bastard!" I shouted and flailed as the acid smoked and burned at my face.

In my thrashing, I spied something lying in the dirt nearby, a pencil that had fallen out of my bag, and scrabbled to reach it while Bugbrain redoubled his efforts to hammer me to death. I took a couple nasty shots to the head and almost blacked out when my skull rebounded off the ground, but crowed in triumph when my hand clasped around the pencil.

I swung blind at Bugbrain and got rewarded with the sick sensation of the pencil bursting through something right before getting splattered with a gush of hot, foul smelling fluid.

Bugbrain flew off me, screaming in pain. I scrabbled away and turned to see him clutching the dripping ruin where an eye used to be. I got to my feet, legs shaking and feeling like I was about to pass out, dripping with muddy green liquid that smelled like rotten, boiled onion.

I made a quick scan of the ground where my bag had fallen, looking for something else to use against the bastard when the screaming stopped.

I looked up, and he was gone.

"That's right, jerk," I laughed and regretted it when my vision dimmed and head began to spin.

I coughed, hacked, and sucked in breaths that felt like my lungs were full of broken glass. The pain was almost overwhelming. The spinning was getting worse and standing was getting difficult so I dropped to my knees. I began fumbling through the dirt, gathering up my things and shoving them back in my bag but my head was pounding and every breath was agony.

I needed help. I picked my cellphone up out of the dirt, an outdated piece of technology, and dialed a number from memory.

"Hello?" A sonorous voice answered after the first ring.

"Swift, it's Thomas. I need your help."

"Thomas? It's been a while. I heard you got eaten by

cockroaches."

"It was just one cockroach, but it was fucking big. Serious man, I need your help. I'm in a bad way." I said, and for a moment the other end went silent.

"Yeah," he said at last, "you usually are. I'll be right there."

I was about to tell him where I was when the line went dead. I frowned and looked at the phone. The jerk had hung up on me.

A fat black crow sitting on top of a nearby dumpster cawed and made me jump. I shot it a sour look, wincing at the movement when my vision went cloudy. I was still looking across at the Other Side of the spectrum which was doing nothing to help my situation. I shifted back to normal and got busy putting my belongings back into my bag.

Most of its contents were mundane enough, like the lifesaving pencils and pens, although I left the gore splattered one in the dirt, and a bunch of battered notebooks. There was a much read and worn copy of Frazer's Golden Bough, the spine of it almost falling apart.

Some other things weren't quite so mundane. I had a

small jar full of salt, a handful of various colored chalk sticks, left-over nubs of multi-colored candles, and quite a few other odds and ends. I liked to be prepared.

I had just gotten the last of it tucked away back in my bag and was settling down to sit and try calling Swift again when the alley exploded with feathers and the thunder of hundreds of wings. I let out a short cry and had about half a heart attack.

If you considered a gathering of crows a murder, what I was looking at was more like an apocalypse, a roiling, cawing cloud of black wings and gleaming beaks, and the sound of it was stunning. And in one singular movement all the birds swung around and stopped. They landed, perched on rooflines, cables, dumpsters, walls, and they all turned their black, beady eyes on me.

"Well this is unnerving as hell." I gulped.

"Don't worry about them. They were just showing me where to find you." Swift emerged from around the corner at the end of the alley.

He looked like something out of an action flick. From his shiny black boots and leather pants, to the sleek black leather jacket encasing his muscular frame, and the mirrored sunglasses, he looked like a living breathing caricature of a Hollywood badass.

"And how did they know where to find me?" I screwed my eyes up at him.

"This one told them, and they told me," he said and stopped at the dumpster where the fat crow that had cawed at me still sat. The bird hopped back and forth on its feet and made a gurgling noise when Swift reached out and patted it on the head, "And now I'm here."

"That is fucking fascinating, man. Think you could help me out? I need to get back to my place but I've recently discovered that my life is in danger, and I'm not quite sure why but I would like to live long enough to find out." I looked up at him, shouldering the strap of my bag and rising to my feet on wobbling legs.

"What kind of guardian angel would I be if I said no?" Swift stepped forward, reaching arms out to steady me, "You look terrible, by the way."

I frowned and shrugged him off, starting to make my way back to the mouth of the alley. I glanced up as all the crows began departing, flying off in every direction. There were so many of them they cast a shadow across the sky.

Swift was a being of many talents and a good example of an Other who wasn't interested in devouring souls or beating hapless folk into the dirt. I had known him for years, worked with him a couple times; he's a good guy to have at your back and altruistic to a fault, guided by some kind of moral code. The guy liked helping people. For free.

He was a rare thing indeed, rarer still for being one of the few people I counted as friend.

"You're not the first one to mention that today. Are we going or what?" I looked back at Swift.

I considered shifting spectrums and getting a look at him but decided against it. I already had a tremendous headache, and every other time I'd caught a glimpse of Swift's true form it was hard to process. Whatever he was behind the shiny human mask, my brain reeled from it on a primitive level.

"Sure, my car's parked in the lot on the other side. Do you need a hand?" Swift offered as he walked to catch up to me.

At my current shambling gait, it only took him a few

strides. I clutched at my bag strap and kept walking.

"I got my ass kicked, I'm not an invalid." I may have snapped.

Swift shrugged it off and walked beside me in silence. We exited the alley and he pointed over to a car parked in front of the coffee shop.

"Serious? That's your car? You're an asshole."

We walked up to it, a solid black '64 GTO that shone in the morning sun like a giant beetle. Even his car looked like something out of a movie. Swift went around to the driver's side and unlocked it; he smiled across the roof of the car at me and slid in. When the lock popped on the passenger side, I opened the door and tossed my bag on the floorboards. I eased my aching self onto the black leather seats, mindful of Bugbrain's ichor still staining my clothes.

"Sorry about the mess," I muttered.

If it bothered Swift, he didn't say a word as he turned the key and the car roared to life, and then we were rumbling out of the parking lot and onto the road.

"Still living in the same place, I take it?" Swift asked, face forward, eyes hidden behind his shades as he drove.

I nodded, sinking into the seat. It was comfortable and I had lost count of how many spots on my body were aching. It was starting to feel like my entire body was one big bruise. I laid my forehead on the cool glass of the window and stared out at the sky as we drove, thinking about what I'd gotten myself into this time.

I must have passed out, because the next thing I remember was the car stopping and Swift killing the engine. I was folded up against the passenger door, drooling on the upholstery. I sat up and stretched, things popped and ground into each other.

"Home." I sighed as I looked out the window

The pounding in my skull had dulled but it was starting to feel like I had a head packed full of cotton. I grabbed my bag and spilled out of the car when Swift came around to open the door but he caught me, propping me up until I could stand on my own two feet. I nodded at him and took a cautious step away, looking up at my humble abode and digging through a pocket for my keys.

"Anybody home?" Swift asked, standing back and staring at my house with a questioning look.

I guess from the outside it might look a bit ramshackle, and a little bit foreboding. I lived out on the outskirts of town along the easternmost city limits, where business and suburbia began fading away into fields, orchards, and dairies. My house sat in the middle of what used to be acres of orchard but was now lots and lots of dirt. Plants refused to take to the soil, the unfortunate by-product of an early dabbling in conjuring that ended in a rather spectacular, if catastrophic, failure.

The only thing that still grew was the massive ash tree my great-grandfather planted over a hundred years ago when he built the house.

Henry Grzeskiewicz, a mage of no small repute in his time, had arrived in America and made his way to California at the dawn of the last century after migrating here from under the shadow of the Tatra Mountains in Poland. He never told anyone what it was that made him pull up roots and move half way around the world, but when he showed up in America the man at the Immigration Department heard the family's original surname and slapped 'Grey' on his papers.

He settled down in the central valley of California after

years of adventure and wandering and built what would become the home to the future generations of the Grey family. Old Henry was probably rolling in his grave at the current state of the place and how much I'd let it go.

It was a fortress, two-stories of grey granite block capped by a heavy black tile roof; Henry built things to last. But the intervening years were hard and now the roof sagged in beneath the ponderous weight of age and it was missing whole patches of tile, even the rugged stones of the walls were stained dark with decades of dust and wear. There were a few windows boarded up; those were my additions after some jerk teenagers busted them out a few years back.

The whole thing looked like it was ready to call it quits and collapse under its own sad weight.

What was I supposed to do? It's only me, and I couldn't keep the electricity running on a regular basis. Scholarly pursuits and shenanigans of an occult nature weren't the most lucrative business field.

"No, Swift," I said as I pulled the key-ring out of my pocket. "There is nobody home."

I went through the half dozen keys and the half dozen locks that studded the heavy steel security door. You can never be too cautious. The hinges let out a dramatic groan as I pushed open the heavy door and turned to look back at Swift, "Come on in, it's totally safe. I'm pretty sure I exorcised all the murder ghosts."

Swift stopped in his tracks behind me and cocked an eyebrow over the rim of his shades. "What?"

"Kidding, kidding," I said and walked inside, hand smacking out and flipping on the lights, "It's possible I missed one."

I didn't catch whatever Swift mumbled as the lights sputtered on. Somewhere down the hall a bulb popped. The inside of my house was in about as poor condition as the outside, but it was harder to tell what with all the stuff crammed into every corner. The front door opened to a spacious foyer that emptied into a long hallway with every available inch of wall space loaded down with bookshelves. Each one was itself crammed to capacity with books of every shape and type; leather bound texts with no discernible title stood side-by-side with books on theoretical physics that leaned against dog-eared paperback fantasies.

Swift's boots clomped along the hardwood flooring as we made our way down the hall.

"Have I ever mentioned you live in a library?" he muttered behind me.

"Yes, well, knowledge is power," I replied and continued down the hall. "Or something."

We cut a corner down the hall and entered the kitchen where a hand-carved wooden edifice of a dinner table surrounded by a half-dozen hand-carved chairs dominated the center of the room, all covered in a grey coating of dust. The hanging cabinets, the fridge, the countertop, everything was grey with dust and cobwebs--except for the microwave

I pretended not to notice many-legged things scuttling into the shadows when I flipped on the light. I don't cook a lot, or entertain guests often. A family hadn't eaten at the table in years.

"Sorry about the mess, I gave the maid the decade off. Wait here, I need to clean myself up," I told Swift as he stood in the middle of the kitchen with his hands tucked in his pockets.

He was still wearing his sunglasses and was looking

around at the room like he expected something to jump out at him.

"Any idea what it is you've gotten yourself into this time?" Swift turned to look at me. "What was it that gave you the thrashing?"

"A really, really big fucking bug. Make yourself comfortable, I'm going to get cleaned up and figure out how to magic up a really, really big fly-swatter."

I ducked out of the kitchen, making for the stairway at the end of the hall that led to the second story and my room. I thought about the thrashing I had taken, as Swift called it. A real magical badass would've annihilated the buzzing bastard in a heartbeat. But I was not what anyone would ever consider a magical badass. My talents ran to other, more subtle things. I mean, yeah, with time and preparation I could make some wild stuff happen, but the force most people call magic is a lot different than movies and books about precocious wizards and magical schools have led the masses to believe.

Which I thought was great because the misdirection makes it easier for people like me and those of my ilk to go unnoticed. When everyone is looking for wands and hocus pocus, they're less likely to notice the decrepit looking fellow whispering secrets out of reality.

I pulled myself up the stairs and entered the second story, passing down a hall of closed doors. I didn't bother flipping on any of the lights as I went, but I'd walked the way so many times the path was pure muscle memory.

I got to the end and pushed the door to my bedroom open, tossing my bag onto my bed, shrugging out of my coat, stumbling through the piles of laundry and precarious stacks of books and other items, pushed open the door to the bathroom and slipped inside.

The fluorescent bulb overhead came on and starting buzzing, the sound grating and making me think of Bugbrain as I went to the shower, cranking the water over to scalding. The pipes rattled and moaned, spitting out a stream of water that took a second to go from murky to clear.

While it warmed up, I went over to the sink to undress and assess my damage in front of the mirror.

"Oh holy shit, that's not right."

Swift neglected to mention the swath of beard that Bugbrain's acid mucous burned off, leaving a patch of red and blistered skin behind. There was a decent sized goose egg rising up on the back of my head when I ran my fingers through my hair and a dark purple bruise was spreading over my side and ribs.

The unfortunate truth is I've been, and looked, worse. For a guy who goes out of his way to be a keep his nose in books and be a hermit, I ended up getting into an unreasonable amount of trouble. Not all secrets hid in the pages of moldering tomes.

Grandpa Grey once said that a mage attracts trouble like horse shit gathers flies, and he was right.

Pain was an unavoidable part of life.

I dug around the cabinet under the sink for my electric clippers and plugged them in while the bathroom was filling up with steam and let my mind wander. Magical folk tended to have a high mortality rate, usually killed off in spectacular displays of power arcane duels, eaten by a nightmare from one of the realms beyond the Other Side, or any number of atrocious fates. It's a large contributor to why there's so few of us to begin with, and why we're spread so thin.

Give a guy amazing, godlike power and he's still going to make stupid decisions and get in over his head. Wizards, warlocks, witches, and worse--we were still only human.

I worked the clippers around my aching skull and watched patches of black hair and beard fall. The more that came off, the more I saw how worked over I'd gotten. Toying with the forces of the Other Side contributed to the demise of my entire family, in one way or another, and was more than likely going to be what did me in.

Not any time soon, if I got that lucky.

Shorn and looking like a naked rat that got chewed on by a Labrador, I stepped under the water of the shower with a hiss. The heat banished errant thoughts, pain shoving my brain into focus. I needed to wrap my head around this whole situation, figure out where the hell Bugbrain came from and who he was working for, track down any leads I could about where the Libro Nihil might be.

If Bugbrain was after it, that meant someone in the shadows did as well, which meant the damn thing was real. Or a whole lot of people were going to get hurt chasing the bogeyman. Either way, if I wanted to get paid I was going to have to get to the bottom of it.

And that would need a fair bit of work as well as pumping some questionable individuals for information. I couldn't shake the feeling that there was something horrible waiting, though, that it was all going to get way worse.

The thing about being paranoid that reality's out to get you and the shadows are full of horrors isn't delusional.

In my experience, it was how you survived.

3

I felt almost sub-human after the shower as I went out and entered the comfortable darkness of my room. I clicked on the reading lamp on my desk and winced at the light. My room was much the same as the rest of the house, a study in chaos and clutter, with the floor hidden under piles of books and boxes containing things that looked like they belonged in a museum or lab.

The bed was a nest, heaped high with pillows and heavy blankets, and there were clothes scattered about all over the floor. I snagged a pair of jeans and a black t-shirt with a picture of a decomposing corpse and an indecipherable band logo on it, both smelling clean, and scooped up my coat as I made my way to my desk to dress.

My desk was a bastion of order amongst madness, my sacred workstation. A massive, heavy wooden edifice with drawers and cabinets built into it that weighed half a ton if it weighed an ounce; I'd had it since I was a kid. I could still remember my dad and grandpa cussing up a storm as they hauled the monstrosity up the stairs and into my room.

I kept the top clear of clutter and debris; the only things on it were a humming computer tower and screen along with a care-worn keyboard and mouse. It was my pride and joy, and where every investigation began and often ended. The evolution of the internet has been an amazing thing, weaving its own kind of magic around the world as it connected distant peoples to a virtual realm of knowledge and information and porn. The internet was as much an invaluable tool to my work as the ancient grimoires and eclectic relics I'd stockpiled over the years.

I pressed the power button on the screen and smiled as it woke up and came to life, glowing at me.

The screen opened up to my email, showing me that a

ton of new messages had arrived while I was out. I perused the senders and frowned at all the junk mail, notifications of replies on message boards and hot bargains at various shopping sites, but stopped when a name stood out from the rest.

Hack Spencer.

That was weird, I hadn't heard from the old man in years. Hack was an old friend of the family, and by old, I mean he was friends with my great-grandfather Henry. If a mage is clever and powerful enough, it was not unheard of for them to cheat death for a couple centuries. It was Hack who took care of me and fostered my growing talents after my parents died and my grandpa disappeared going on twenty years ago. He was like another grandfather, but we'd had a falling out a while back, an extreme difference of opinions, and hadn't spoken since.

Hack reaching out to me after all this time got me curious, and a little worried. He made it quite clear the last time we spoke that he wanted nothing to do with me, "and my god damn foolishness," and that was that.

I made some stupid, selfish decisions and used my powers in ways that could've had cataclysmic repercussions. If Hack was contacting me, something was wrong, and the subject line on the email confirmed it: Red Sky at Morning.

"Sailors take warning," I muttered to myself.

It was something Hack used to say when times got bad; it meant a storm was coming. I started getting anxious. This was a bad sign, first Devlin and the Libro Nihil and now this. Hack was a survivor. I never figured out how old he was but any mage who survived as long as he had control of a frightening degree of power. I'd gotten to see him cut loose a few times back in the day when I was a kid. It was impressive, and scary as hell.

What could be so bad he needed my help?

I got dressed and stomped into my boots, sitting down and clicking on the email the bad news.

Tommy,

I hate these stupid machines.

Sorry it's been so long, boy. I wish there was time to explain things to you but time's the one thing we're all in short supply of. I just hope you can believe I'm sorry for the way things ended between us.

There's a shadow hanging over the valley, maybe you no-

ticed. It's bringing doom with it and I can't stop the thing by myself, it's too damn powerful. Meet me soon as you can, I'm back in town and I'll be waiting for you at Grannok's Cell.

We don't have much time.

The Sleeper Awakens.

- Hack

That last line sent cold, dead fingers down my spine and left a bad taste in my mouth.

Last I heard, Hack was roaming along the West Coast doing god only knew what. The whole message reeked of ominous portents, what with all the doom and shadows and whatever the hell the Sleeper was. Hack wasn't the sort to exaggerate, so as usual I assumed the worst: he was telling the truth and the shit was in great peril of colliding with the fan.

More and more I was beginning to regret getting out of bed today, but Devlin and his sweet promises of payday were tempting. Things were starting to pile on thick, and I had no idea where to even begin. I needed to get on top of figuring out the situation with the Libro Nihil, but if something as bad as Hack claimed was on its way to the valley, the book would have to wait.

It was still early; I had lots of daylight left, which was a concept that was alien and would take getting used to.

I shut down the computer, snagged my bag, and hurried downstairs, meandering through the halls to the kitchen where I'd left Swift.

Much to my surprise, he was standing right where I left him, as if he hadn't moved the entire time.

"What the hell are you doing?" I stopped in the doorway and asked.

A shiver ran through his body and he turned to face me, like he was coming out of a trance. He shook his head, reaching up and taking off his glasses as he did. He rubbed at his eyes with the heel of a hand and I gawked.

His eyes were solid white, no iris, no pupil; solid, empty white like polished bone.

He caught me looking and slipped his shades back on with a frown.

"Sorry, I was thinking." He shrugged and looked me up and down. "You look less terrible."

"Thanks?" I stepped into the kitchen and looked up at

him. “What the hell is up with your eyes, man?”

Swift stood up straighter and folded his arms across his chest, which made me notice how much larger and imposing he was. His frown deepened and he tilted his head at me, letting his sunglasses slip down his nose some to expose a glimpse of his eyes, which were a normal, boring shade of hazel.

“My eyes?” Swift asked.

I grumbled. More hidden depths to the enigma that was Swift, that I would get to the bottom of someday, when doom and shadows and evil books weren’t about to lay waste to my life.

“Time to go.” I turned on my heel and called back over my shoulder as I went down the hall, “We’re going to the Bastille.”

“Why are we going to a night club at nine in the morning?”

“The end of the world, of course. I’ll fill you in on the way.”

I was stiff and sore but functional as we made our way outside. A breeze had picked up, carrying with it a sharp autumn chill, and I zipped up my coat before turning to secure all the locks on the door. Swift, of course, showed no signs of discomfort as he went for his car.

After we'd gotten into Swift's car and were heading down the road to town, I filled Swift in on Hack's letter. He listened without saying a word, eyes straight ahead the whole time.

"And Grannok's Cell is?" Swift asked when I finished.

"Abel Grannok was a farmer around a hundred years ago. He also happened to be a mage of no small talent and a dangerous psychopath," I said. Swift perked up at that, but kept his eyes on the road, so I continued, "According to the story, he had been communing with some of the uglier denizens of the Other Side for a while and working on ways to bring one over and devour its essence. He thought he could achieve apotheosis--godhood, right?--by consuming an elder being. My great-grandfather Henry, along with my mentor Hack, who were, like, a couple old timey magical badasses, went after him when folks around town started to go missing.

They found him at his farm in the middle of opening a portal to some hideous nightmare realm on the Other Side, surrounded by the ritually slaughtered remains of a couple dozen victims. Fucked up, right? The entity was already making its way through when Henry and Hack disrupted the ritual, closing the portal and binding Grannok with sundry magics, but the reflux of energies fried the bastard's mind and left him a gibbering idiot. Back then, the Bastille was an actual prison. Bastille's French for prison, see? Hanford's classy. Also explains all the brick and iron architecture. Anyways. They locked Grannok away in one of the cells, but one night an angry mob of townsfolk broke in. They believed the Devil possessed Grannok, and went in loaded down with pitchforks, torches, and the like. They were furious about all the victims, with good reason.

So, right there in the cell, they strung him up and hung him, beat him, then lit him on fire. There wasn't a damn thing he could do about it, the man's mind was gone, but the people didn't care. They just wanted justice, some kind of closure. I can't blame them. But, long story short, the reason it's called Grannok's Cell, is because his ghost still haunts it."

I took in a deep gulp of air after finishing the story. Grannok's Cell underneath the Bastille also happened to be where Hack took me once upon a time to practice the more dangerous aspects of being a mage. Evocation, lethal forces, stuff like that.

He used to say it was shielded from outside influences, or something. Might be why he wanted to meet there.

"Grannok haunts his old cell?" Swift turned the car onto one of the streets that led downtown, the story having eaten up most the trip.

The Bastille was in the civic square, by the old courthouse and an ice cream parlor in a little park area. There was an antique carousel ringed with fantastical creatures nearby, and right across the street was an old abandoned theater. The library was spitting distance away, too. Most of the buildings in the downtown area were damn near decrepit, ancient things that the city liked to call historic, but they had lots of stories to tell.

"Not sure. I've never seen Grannok, but the whole building hums with power and activity from the Other Side." I said as we pulled into the parking lot beside the Bastille.

In this part of town were a lot of old growth trees, towering valley oaks and mulberries, and they kept the red brick building in a state of near-perpetual shade. Though the place had gone through many renovations and owners since its construction a couple centuries back, the Bastille still looked like a prison. There were towers at each corner, crenellations along the curtain walls and the iron bars on all the windows.

Recently, as Swift said, it had been converted into Hanford's trendiest nightclub.

I snagged my bag and Swift and I got out of the car. We walked around the building to the front, passing by a cluster of city landscapers maintaining the grounds around the square. By the grand stone water fountain, a pack of old men sat at a picnic table, drinking from bottles in brown bags and playing checkers.

It was so normal it made me wince.

To the casual observer, life as usual, another quiet day in a quiet town. We walked up the steps of the Bastille and approached two massive oaken doors studded with iron rivets, and I glanced up at the unlit neon sign hanging above them proclaiming the building's new moniker.

"Nightside? Seriously?" I pounded on the door with a balled fist.

"I think they're closed, Thomas," Swift said from behind me.

"There's always someone here, even if there's not."

Swift was about to say something but I held up a hand for silence, right as one of the heavy doors swung open of its own accord. Inside everything was dark except where the sun cut through the iron bars on the windows, revealing the main floor of the club in slashes of shadow and light.

It was a great empty space, I assumed a dance floor/ It had an area with high-top tables and a bar off to one side that took up a majority of the far wall, and a large stage on the other. In the back, by the restrooms, was an unmarked door tucked into the corner.

"Don't be so cryptic." Swift said from behind me as we stepped inside.

I waggled my fingers in the air. "I'm a wizard, man; I'm allowed to be cryptic."

We had made it about halfway across when the front door shut itself with a hollow thud that echoed through the room. I cringed a little, looking back to see Swift standing at the ready with his hands raised up and curled into fists.

"Calm down, the caretaker knows me. We're probably safer in here than we were outside," I told Swift and continued walking.

"That's comforting. Who's the caretaker?" Swift asked.

"What." I approached the unmarked door at the back of the room and clasped the handle. It opened up to a short dark hallway and I flipped the light switches on the nearby wall.

"Who's the caretaker?" Swift asked again.

"I heard you the first time. What is the caretaker, not who. What." I passed by the first two doors in the hallway when the overhead lights came on. At the back were two flights of stairs opposing each other, one leading up and the other leading down. I took the one leading down.

"Why does working with you always give me a headache?" Swift's boots echoed in the small stairwell.

"Maybe I'm just too much for you to handle," I said with a shrug. I kept my hand on the wall as we went down, counting steps along the way, "I get that a lot."

My skull started humming as soon as we walked into the Bastille but I chalked it up to the building itself. But every step down into its guts it got worse, more insistent, until it was a nagging whine inside my head once we got to the bottom of the stairs.

I spotted a cord dangling from a bay of overhead lights and yanked on it, illuminating what looked like a cramped, crumbling prison cellblock, which made sense considering that was what it used to be. There was row after row of cells fronted by sturdy, black iron bars. They were all serving as wine cellars and storage these days, crammed with racks of bottles and boxes of supplies.

Swift snorted. "I can still kick your ass." He looked around at the place. "So which one's Grannok's?"

"Don't threaten me with a good time, sir." I pointed down to the end of the row where the lights didn't quite reach, where the shadows seemed to pool and cling to everything.

I took a breath, switching between spectrums, and it all changed.

I could see luminous white vapor rising out of the cells and coalescing into the spectral shapes of men and women, or the echoes of men and women, hazy individuals floating about with no direction. They weren't even proper ghosts, harmless specters at best, and they dispersed as I walked through them. It tingled when I did, and I caught snags and fragments of memories that weren't mine.

I saw someone crying in a courtroom, a bright afternoon in spring on horseback, the blank look on my wife's face as I held her underwater.

I shook off the thoughts, banishing the dead memories, and pressed on. When we got close to the last cell, I noticed something seeping across the floor, red and slick.

There was blood everywhere, a lot of it.

Things aren't supposed to bleed that much. I rushed over to the cell door and skidded to a stop when I saw what was inside.

"God damn it," I gasped.

It was Hack.

He lay curled up on the floor of the cell, trying to hold his insides from spilling out of the great gash that split his belly open. He looked terrible, and much smaller than I remembered. The Hack I knew was a giant, vibrating with power and the poor creature in front of me was a shriveled up husk of a man. From the countless wrinkles to the patches of liver spots and ropey veins standing up beneath tissue-paper skin, he looked ancient, half-dead already.

“It’s too late,” I said, dropping to my knees beside the broken man and lifting a hand to wipe away the blood that stained his face and matted down his beard, when his hand shot up and wrapped around my wrist like a vice, grinding bones together.

I gasped and heard Swift cry out behind me. Hack yanked me down and pressed his face up against mine, eyes wide open and bloodshot, pupils swallowing up all the color.

“Not too late,” he rasped.

4

"He's alive?" Swift exclaimed.

I was going to answer when Hack went limp, releasing his grip on my wrist and falling slack in my arms. His breath was slow and shallow and his skin was pale. I looked down at the gaping wound in his abdomen where he still had one arm clutching at his own intestines, and my eyes went wide when I noticed something curious about it. With my vision shifted, I could see faint wisps of light flickering and moving along the edges of the wound, sparkling with curious energies, so I leaned in for a closer look.

The flesh was growing back before my eyes, trying to pull itself together. It was like watching a fractal in slow motion, expanding, replicating, at some point he even stopped bleeding out.

"Yeah, somehow. He's fighting, but we have to get him out of here; whatever attacked him is more than likely still around here somewhere." I pulled my jacket off, maneuvering Hack's limp body enough to get it wrapped and tied off around his midsection in an improvised bandage. " Give me a hand."

I got my arms under Hack's shoulders and started lifting when Swift moved around to help.

I caught a glimpse of him in his true form and froze up, almost dropping Hack. His body was a solid humanoid shape of perfect white with frail looking elongated limbs composed of ethereal light. Searing luminescence fanned out from his back, looking like a pair of massive wings. Something in my brain popped, I gasped, and feared my grey matter would start leaking out my nose. I scrambled to drag my sight back across the spectrum while my brain screeched.

"We have to move." Swift cast a grave look at me from

where he stood supporting Hack, looking normal again.

I nodded and took a second to catch my breath and compose myself before Swift and I each got an arm under Hack's shoulders and lifted him from the ground. We made our way slowly, careful not to slip in the puddle of blood, and began making our way to the stairwell.

I kept sneaking glances over at Swift while my brain spun trying to process what the hell it was I saw. I don't think I ever got such a direct look at him from the Other Side before. I've seen a lot of bizarre, terrifying, beautiful, and downright confusing things since I awoke to my talents and the wider world. But looking at Swift in his true form was the rough metaphysical equivalent of staring at the sun through a magnifying glass.

Someday soon I was going to have to come out and ask him about it.

Swift stopped and looked over at me. " Let me carry him, it'll be easier."

I let go and Swift slung Hack's body up to cradle him in his arms like the old man weighed nothing. With a shrug, I took the lead and made my way back to the stairs. We had made it about halfway up when a huge sound from above stopped both of us in our tracks. It sounded like something had torn through part of the building, a thunderous booming and shattering followed by a familiar metallic squeal.

“Bugbrain!” I began to jog up the steps and Swift followed suit, even burdened by Hack.

I tore through the door to the stairwell and down the short hallway, slamming straight through the door to the main floor, and skidded to a stop when I came out the other side, my jaw dropping open at the remarkable sight that waited in the main room.

Trudging its way across the dance floor was a golem towering somewhere over ten or twelve feet high, its body constructed from chunks of the Bastille itself. It had the shape of a man, in that it had two arms and two legs, but made of bricks and mortar, wood and pipe, studded with jagged shards of broken glass. The floor and a piece of the wall near the stage were gone, material to fuel the creation.

“What is that thing supposed to be?” Swift came up alongside me and asked.

“That would be the caretaker.” I nodded in the golem’s direction.

I peeked at the Other Side as Bugbrain screeched and launched himself out from the shadows, a pair of undersized wings buzzing on his back, head lopsided now with one bulbous eye missing. I felt a flash of pride at that. His proboscis was spraying acid spit everywhere, leaving sizzling holes wherever the nasty stuff landed.

Some of it hit the caretaker but it didn’t slow down a bit; instead, it swung a massive, club-like arm out and caught the bastard in midair, sending him flying to crash into the bar.

I caught a closer look at the caretaker and saw the hazy, vaporous forms of the specters from below, surrounding it in a swirling nimbus. I spared a hasty glance at Swift.

“We need to get out of here, they’re making a lot of--” I got cut off when a shriek tore through the din of the fight, and swung around to look at the front doors where it came from.

Standing inside the doorway was a woman pushing a cart loaded down with mops, brooms, rags, bottles, and other assorted cleaning implements. She looked to be on the far side of middle-aged, forty-something, had brown skin and dark hair pulled back in a severe bun, and harsh, sharp features with large black almond-shaped eyes. She stood maybe a couple inches over five feet and wore a pair of drab blue coveralls over a sturdy frame. I could make out a nametag over her left breast that read, 'Rosa.'

She was also still screaming.

Bugbrain pulled himself out of the wreckage of the bar and spun the face the cleaning lady. He saw his chance and took it, making a break for her and the door beyond. From her point of view, she must have thought she was about to get railroaded by an insane geriatric.

The caretaker swung itself around and made to go after Bugbrain but was too slow. Things were going to get messy in a hurry if someone didn't do something and Swift was still busy holding Hack's limp body.

I jammed a hand into my bag and grasped the first thing I found, a piece of chalk as big as my finger, and yanked it out. I gritted my teeth, but it would have to do.

I reached inside of myself for my power, the magic that flowed through me, pulling on the energy that filled the Bastille as well, feeling it coursing through me like the echo of a roaring wave. I didn't have time for anything fancy, I could only pour everything I had into one shot, and I threw the chalk at Bugbrain as hard as I could while releasing the energy along with it.

The chalk tore out of my hand like a comet, moving so fast it burst into blue flames and left a shimmering tail of light behind it. The tiny ball of fire ripped straight through Bugbrain and buried itself in the brick wall behind him. He hit the ground and slid right up to the cleaning lady's feet, a smoldering hole punched through his chest.

Rosa the cleaning lady stared down at Bugbrain's still twitching, smoking body, her eyes wide with shock and mouth working like a landed fish, but no more screams came out.

The little display left me feeling hollowed out and my head was spinning as I sagged against a convenient wall nearby, waiting for my vision to stop wavering in and out.

Blowing through that much energy all at one time drained me, and was a stupid damn thing to do. That was why we wizarding types have things like formulas and rituals, tools and other crazy magical paraphernalia, things to amplify and focus the energy we poured out of ourselves. A mage's ability comes from his connection to the universal force that moves all things, what most tended to call magic.

But to take too much from it without something to focus it through, or make a blatant distortion of reality's laws, can burn you out. And pulling a stunt that played as fast and loose with the laws of physics as what I did took a lot of juice.

"That was cool," Swift said.

"No, it was stupid." I pushed myself off the wall, moving with shaking legs.

The caretaker made a groaning noise as pieces of it began flying off and moving to their original places, soon the room began looking more normal. Even the bar that Bugbrain crashed through was putting itself back together.

I looked over at where Rosa the cleaning lady still stood and had started trembling as she looked straight at me.

"We need to get out of here." I hurried over to the door.

On the ground beside Rosa, Bugbrain's body began curling in on itself. After a second, the whole thing collapsed into a heap of black dust. I stomped through it and up to the cleaning lady. She was still staring at me, watching every movement, her left eye twitching.

"All right, lady. Rosa, right? You have to come with us, it's not safe here. Okay?" I tried to sound comforting, but it must not have worked too well because she took a swing at me, "Hey!"

Swift was there, holding Hack against him; he brushed his hand across Rosa's cheek and she dropped in an unconscious heap. I stared down at her, then back up to Swift who was already making his way out the doors.

I thought for a moment about just leaving her there, but there was no way of knowing if any friends of Bugbrain were hanging around, and the cops were bound to show up sooner or later considering how much noise the scuffle caused. And cops asked a lot of questions. Rosa may not understand what she saw, but word has a weird way of getting around, and someone might be able to piece something together.

Not to mention she had gotten a good look at Swift and I. The only sensible thing was to take her and figure out what to do about it later, so I tried lifting her and failed. I felt wasted from burning too much energy.

"This is brilliant," I muttered and looked around, noticing Rosa's cleaning cart.

In a pinch, it would do. I kicked all the cleaning utensils off it which left me with a decent sized flat space onto which I managed to manhandle Rosa. She didn't fit well; her arms were dangling over the side and her head was a precarious distance from a wheel, but she wasn't in any shape to complain.

Grabbing the handles to the cart, I pushed her out the door and tried as best as I could to be inconspicuous as I rolled an unconscious woman along the sidewalk of the civic square and out to the parking lot. One of the old men by the water fountain gave me a curious look but said nothing, and we made it to safety behind the building where I could already hear the rumble of Swift's car. We came around the corner and he got out to help me stuff Rosa into the backseat alongside Hack before we jumped in.

Hack was already beginning to look better, which was odd given that a few minutes ago he was knocking on death's door, some of the color returning to his skin and his breathing was even and steady. Rosa fell against him, and began snoring gently.

Somewhere nearby I could hear sirens, but they were a worry. We were a ways down the road when Swift finally spoke up.

“So what’s the deal with the cleaning lady?” he asked.

“As of right now I have no clue. I’m more worried about how Bugbrain knew where Hack was, and what he knows that’s so damned important.” I kept watching the buildings and cars go by out the window.

As much as I worried about Hack and my deteriorating day, Rosa the cleaning lady was going to be a wrench in the gears if I didn’t settle on something to do about her. It’s not like I could erase her memory and dump her on the side of the road somewhere, which would be wrong.

It didn’t even bear thinking on.

Much.

5

The drive away from the Bastille was quiet except for Rosa sleeping in the back seat. She snored and mumbled in Spanish and every once in a while would let out a burst of what I assumed to be curses.

A few times I glanced over at Swift as he drove but the image of that bright being of light still haunted the edges of my vision, so I'd look out the window to try and think but end up getting dizzy watching everything go by.

I was going to be low for a while after the nonsense I pulled, as evidenced by the dull throbbing between my eyes. So far, today had been a complete train wreck. I had more questions than I did to begin with, the mystery kept getting deeper, and I felt like I'd taken a beating--which I had.

At the rate I was going, I was going to wind up dead by sundown.

I decided as we pulled up to my place that I wasn't going anywhere else until I figured out what the hell was going on, not to mention take a handful of aspirin. Not having answers made me feel weak and hopeless and I was more than capable of making myself feel that way without any extra help, but right then I had no answers at all.

And that would get me killed quick as anything.

"Come on, we can put Hack up in my parent's old room," I told Swift after he killed the engine. "Then come back for Rosa."

He complied and got Hack out of the back seat, hoisting the unconscious old man up into his arms as easy as before. I glanced over at Rosa, who had sunken down into a heap on the car seat when Swift moved Hack out. She looked so peaceful that I was a bit jealous, despite the drool working its way out of her mouth.

I walked ahead of Swift to get the front door open and led the way up the stairs to the second floor, turning on lights as we went and opening the door across the hall from mine.

“Right in there, on the bed.” I stepped aside to make way.

Dim light crept into the room from behind heavy curtains on the windows, disturbing dust that had accumulated for years. White drop cloths blanketed the room, draped over the bed and furniture. I chuckled a bit; in the limpid half-light, it looked like everything had dressed up in cheap ghost costumes, but the laugh died quickly.

I hadn’t been in my parent’s room since after they died. I began shuffling, feeling uncomfortable as I looked around at all their things covered in white. Swift laid Hack on the bed and he sunk into it with a quiet groan.

“Can you get the cleaning lady? I’ll check on him.” I looked sideways at Swift as I spoke. “We can stick her on the couch downstairs I guess. When will she wake up from that voodoo you put her under?”

“When I want her to,” Swift said as he left the room.

I set my bag down and gave Hack the once over. He

somehow managed to look even better than he did in the car, color returning to his cheeks, skin seeming to smooth out. Magic, it did a body good.

I worked my coat from around his midsection and noticed with surprise that it wasn't soaked through with blood. It was disgusting and I would have to burn it, but it wasn't caked with gore. I dropped it on the floor beside the bed and went back to examining Hack. When he got attacked, he was wearing a pair of slacks and a faded sweater, both now soiled and shredded.

Through the rags of his sweater, I could see his midsection and got another surprise. What should have been a gaping, bloody hole was instead a stomach with angry, red scar tissue spread across it in a jagged line.

That went well beyond magical and bordered on the miraculous.

Last I checked, spontaneous regeneration wasn't on the list of often crazy things a mage could do. I was going to have to interrogate the old man on many things when he finally came to.

I heard the front door shut and after a minute Swift was standing at the door to my parent's room.

He leaned against the doorjamb and watched me. "Lady's on the couch, you want me to wake her up?"

I shook my head and began the onerous task of getting Hack out of his ruined clothes. As I did, I began noticing more scars like the one now on his stomach, but smooth and faded by time. After I had him undressed and a pile of ruined, bloody garments on the floor, I pulled the cloth covering the bed over him. I stood up straight and my back popped in resentment.

"One thing at a time, man. You said she wouldn't wake up till you made her, right?" I made my way past Swift and out of the room.

"Right. What next, then?"

"Exactly what I need to figure out, before this day goes even more to hell. I'm considering giving Devlin a call and asking if he knows about any shady newcomers in town."

We made it to the kitchen and I flipped the lights on and went to get myself a glass of water. Some vestigial remnant of manners made me get one for Swift, too.

"That could be a long list. You're talking about Hanford, there's a whole lot of shady to go around these days." Swift made his way to the table and swung a chair out to straddle it backwards.

"Yeah but right now it's all I got, and near as I remember none of the locals are in the Armageddon business." I sat down across from him and slid one of the cups over. "Sure there's some real nasty motherfuckers in need of an old fashioned stomping but there haven't been any true blue world enders since the Broken Circle got the boot."

Between gross mistreatment of my skull and its contents by an angry bug person and tampering with volatile forces, my head was full of static, which was making it difficult to form coherent thoughts. So the two of us sat at the table in a growing, uncomfortable silence, staring at our glasses.

"I've never seen you do anything like that trick with the chalk. It was pretty cool." Swift looked up from his glass.

"Sure, but it damn near wiped me out." I looked across the table at Swift with a frown. "There's a reason I don't do nonsense like that unless I have to."

"You saved the cleaning lady, though, that counts for something right?"

I shrugged. "Sure? Only because it was easier than cleaning up the mess Bugbrain would've made out of her." I watched Swift's face fall into a heavy frown.

Not the answer he was expecting.

"You can't be serious," he said.

"Of course I am. We puny mortals make great big messes. You can't tell me it wouldn't be easier to wipe her memory and dump her back at the--what?" Swift's jaw had fallen slack as he looked at me in disbelief.

"You had better be joking, Thomas."

I blinked and drummed my fingers on the tabletop. "Of course I'm joking. I would never do anything like that, but we do need to deal with her." I cleared my throat and rose from the table.

Swift was giving me a disapproving look from over the rims of his shades. I couldn't believe he was giving me so much grief, it wasn't like I suggested we kill the lady and bury her out back--I was in no shape for digging holes, not after the morning I'd had.

We left the kitchen, Swift following me down the hall to the living room. I don't think it counted as a living room anymore considering there hadn't been much living done in it in a long time. Like my parents' bedroom and every other room in the place except mine, white drop-cloths were everywhere, obscuring the shapes of the furniture. The big blocky shapes up against the walls were the antique china cabinets that my father had spent most his life filling to the brim with the oddities and trophies he collected during his travels around this and other worlds.

Dad had moonlighted as an anthropology professor at the big university up north when he wasn't busy scouring the far realms of the Other Side and managed to amass quite a collection.

Rosa the cleaning lady sprawled out on the massive sofa-shaped white thing in front of the stone fireplace, her mouth open in mid-snore.

I dragged the footstool from under a nearby armchair over, sat it in front of the couch and took a seat. Swift stood at the end of the couch near Rosa's head and looked over at me.

"Ready?" he asked.

I took a breath and a moment to compose myself. There was no way around it, this was going to suck.

I nodded to Swift. "Yeah fuck it, man. Go for it."

He reached a hand down and ran it across Rosa's cheek, then skirted around the couch and stepped behind me. A rapid sequence of events followed: she sat up, her eyes flew open and she threw a wild look around the room before spotting me, and then her face hardened, twisting into a vicious scowl.

If I didn't know better, I'd say there was murder gleaming in her wide, dark eyes. I was familiar with the look. She flew off the couch in a blur and tackled me.

"Brujo!" Rosa hollered the word like a battle-cry and so began my second assault of the day.

She was strong and fast. She landed a solid blow on my jaw that left my ears ringing before I could grab her wrists and struggle to not get my brains beaten out. Swift swooped around and plucked Rosa off me. He held her at arm's length where she clawed and hissed like a cat, belting through a blistering string of curses and profanities in Spanish.

"Swift, damn it man put her out already!" I picked myself up off the ground, rubbing my throbbing jaw. It went well with my running collection of head trauma.

Rosa went limp mid-shout when Swift laid his hand on

her cheek and he dumped her in a heap back on the couch.

"Maybe we should wipe her memory and dump her in a cornfield." Swift looked down at Rosa, who had transformed into a peaceful, snoring puddle on the couch.

"Damn Tommy, you always did have a way with women," a voice like gravel rumbled from nearby.

I looked over to the hallway where Hack stood. He had cleaned most the blood off and wrapped the white sheet from the bed around him into an improvised toga, and was leaning up against the wall with his arms folded over his grizzled chest and a toothy smile on his face. His eyes were bright, clear, and a dazzling shade of solid blue like iridescent sapphires.

This was new and strange and added another question to my growing list.

"You and me, boy, we need to talk. For starters, you mind telling me what you got a damn angel of death doing in your house?" Hack squinted across the room at Swift with his glowing blue eyes.

"Talk about what now?" My head was starting to hurt worse.

I looked over my shoulder at Swift who was standing in front of the fireplace like a statue, arms folded over his chest and his mouth set in a flat line. Whatever was going on behind those mirrored lenses, it didn't look like he was about to start talking.

I looked back at Hack, who had come into the living room and was peeking under the cloths on the furniture.

"Okay, more on whatever that's supposed to mean in a second," I moved across the room to stand in front of Hack. "Mind telling me what's up with the shiny magic eyes? They didn't look like that earlier, old man."

Despite those crazy eyes, he looked almost exactly like he did the last time we spoke. Yelled, the last time we yelled. That was what six, no, seven years ago now? He was still Hack, though, despite everything else.

He still looked like a mean, short Santa Claus what with that giant white prospector's beard.

"Yeah, yeah I suppose I might owe you some answers. Make me some coffee, and I'll tell you everything," Hack grumbled.

It was disturbing, looking him eye-to-eye. I felt my heart

swell up and the current of magic inside me stir as something within those eyes pulled at it.

"Sorry, all out." I took a step back and looked away.

And he stepped forward, pushing a blunt finger in my chest. "Then make some, boy."

Make some?

Years of silence and the old man still wanted to push me, to test me. My parents had raised me to study the world, to be a scholar and use my brain, to observe the hidden truths of reality.

When they died and Hack took over as my caretaker and mentor, all that changed. My life turned into boot camp. We drilled every day on manipulating esoteric forces and how to distort reality, manipulating it to achieve unbelievable things.

Hack was the last of a dying breed, a holdover of the old-school spell slingers from a time before reality had begun calcifying and paradigms got wiped out wholesale by altering beliefs. He told me once it wasn't that magic was dying or fading, but that ever-growing humanity's belief was cutting it off and building a wall around the world.

He was a hard teacher, heavy-handed, and he didn't

abide failure. Hack had outlived almost everyone he ever knew, and to him failure often equated to death.

"Well?" Hack asked, waiting, watching me.

"Whatever. I'll do your little monkey dance." I turned to go get my bag from upstairs. "But then you're spilling your guts."

"Wouldn't be the first time today," Hack called out behind me.

6

We all met up in the kitchen once I'd gotten my bag and found Hack a pair of sweats and a flannel to wear. He was stockier than me and the clothes ended up fitting on the tight side but it was better than the sheet-toga.

I rummaged around in the trash for a second and dug out the empty coffee tin, placing it in the center of the table while Hack and Swift watched, and then fished a decent sized piece of white chalk out of my bag.

"Place ain't looking too good these days, boy," Hack grumbled as he watched me work. "You ain't looking too good, either."

"Well it ain't been sunshine and puppy dogs around here since you bailed," I spat back without looking up as I went about preparing my workspace. "Hanford, the whole valley, it's getting darker, uglier. Now could you shut up so I can work?"

There were as many ways to bend reality and work magic as there were practitioners of the arcane. The most blatant and dangerous way was to bludgeon the laws of nature and distort them beyond recognition. The chalk-comet stunt I pulled at the Bastille was a perfect example: accelerating a mundane object to incredible speed and endowing it with lethal force. It all looks super cool on film and is devastating, as the late Bugbrain could attest, but reality didn't appreciate such indelicate treatment.

It comes back on the offending mage with a vengeance and I got off lucky with only a headache to show for it; mucking about with forces on that level, completely unprepared, could've blown my head off.

Seriously, though.

The more sensible and reliable method was much preferred by a mortality-conscious mage such as myself. It involved manipulating the flow of the universe's unifying force, that tricky little thing called magic, and paradigms through rituals, sly and subtle like instead of hauling off and demanding miracles from nature.

It all sounds even stuffier and ridiculous on paper, the kind of thing old timey wizards would pack dusty tomes with to put their apprentices to sleep. But it damn well works, and has a much higher survival rate. And that is why I busied myself with chalking out the prerequisite magical shapes and scribbles around the coffee tin that would allow me to focus the necessary energies.

To the uninitiated, it looked like I was scribbling all over the table.

"That's an awful lot of nonsense," Swift whispered.

"Hush, you." I kept my eyes on my work, adding sigils and flourishes here and there.

Hack grunted and shot a wary look across the table at Swift before turning his attention back to me. I could feel his scrutiny like an actual weight pressed against me but I was getting to the tricky part, the important part, and shoved it and everything else from my mind as I gathered my focus.

I shifted spectrums so that I could perceive the subtle fluctuations of energy all around me, the current of magic, the sleepy grey aura of power that hung around the house from generations of mages honing and working their craft. I raised my hands and held them flat in the air above the table, watching as the chalk lines flickered with threads of ghost light I focused on giving reality a nudge.

For thousands of years, mages, will-workers, wizards, shamans, and the like have all known a fundamental truth that modern science is beginning to grasp, the fact that matter is energy in a static, defined form. If a person were able to perceive the flow of that energy all around them, underlying the fabric of creation, and manipulate it, they could alter and control that flow.

They could work magic.

In my mind's eye, I could see atoms spinning in an intricate dance, mirroring stars in galactic orbits, all dancing together and weaving a universal tapestry. And I thought of a strong cup of coffee on a cold winter morning, its warmth and smell and taste.

The lines of chalk on the table began glowing more and a haze coalesced and swirled inside the coffee tin as I stoked the spark of power inside myself and gathered my will, drawing in a deep breath.

I held my breath, my power, and as I did, the world changed. The gentlest wave of distortion spread out into creation along with my breath when I exhaled. The lines and shapes on the table flared a color that was all colors, from grey to a rippling rainbow, the haze in the tin shimmering and solidifying. Stars blossomed before my eyes and my head spun, then I dropped back into the normal spectrum to see my work and there on the table sat a full tin of dark brown coffee, where once it was empty.

Behold my power and tremble ye mortals, coffee ex nihilo.

"There, you old bastard." I turned to look at Hack; he was looking at me with his arms folded over his chest and a small smile on his face. "Happy?"

"Not bad, not bad." Hack nodded "Guess you'll want some answers, now."

"Damn right, now sit down and get talking."

I picked up the coffee, went over to the derelict electric coffee maker hiding in the shadows of the counter and began the mundane ritual of making a fresh pot. I'm pretty sure Hack couldn't have cared less about a hot cup, he just wanted to gauge my abilities since the last time we'd seen each other. Before he left, a working like that, recreating a memory, would've taken me the whole day to pull off, and a lot more energy. I'd gotten better since then, more efficient, at harnessing and manipulating magic. Made me wonder why I didn't try it when I first ran out of coffee.

"Sure, but not with that here." Hack was glaring across the table at Swift.

For his part, Swift sat motionless in his chair, eyes hidden behind his shades and face neutral as stone. But the tension between them was palpable like the pressure in the air before a lightning strike.

"I am surrounded by children." I pulled a mug down from the cabinet and smacked it onto the countertop with a sharp bang. Hack and Swift both turned to look at me. "I've known you a while now Swift, and out of professional courtesy and some weird sense of friendship I've never dug into your business, but that shit earlier, with the light, and the burning, and the whatever the fuck you are? It scared the willies out of me. You hear me? The god damn willies."

The two of them were looking at me like I'd grown a second head. I stood there tapping my foot, waiting for someone to start talking.

Something in Swift's face cracked and he turned to stare down at the tabletop while Hack flashed a smug grin at me, his eyes catching the light.

"Swear to god, boy. You ain't got any sense, do you? He's Malakhim." Hack said it like it explained everything.

"Swift's a lot of things but an angel is not one of them. Besides, the entity known as Jehovah fragmented into splinters eons ago. He's not schizophrenic enough to be one of its servants." I frowned, looking from Hack to Swift.

The old man was about to speak when Swift looked up and took off his glasses, laying them on the table and revealing his eyes had once again become the empty white voids I had seen earlier.

I groaned. I was in a room full of guys with freaky in-human eyes and questionable intent. Hack snapped his mouth shut and started to get out of his seat, but Swift raised a hand and turned to look at me. What little light was in the kitchen began to blossom, growing and spreading until the whole room filled with an otherworldly radiance as Swift stood.

"Malakhim is only one of the names the Children of Dust have given us across millennia. We do not serve the Broken God; we are messengers of forces that far pre-date this iteration of reality. I mean you no harm and never have Thomas. Question no further lest you endanger yourself and your sanity, it is not yet time for the answers to these questions. But know if I had wished your destruction, you would have as much hope stopping me as an ant standing against the sun. The old vessel knows this; it is why he fears me." Swift's voice rang like a bell that vibrated in my bones and through the stones of the house.

And it scared the living shit out of me.

Hack had gotten to his feet, a nimbus of crackling light growing around his upraised hands, his eyes burning like flares. There was a sick little part of me that wanted to see what would happen if the two of them went head-to-head but I was pretty sure it would end in the worst way possible--particularly for me and my home.

I did the first thing that came to mind and slung the pot of coffee that had just finished brewing across the kitchen where it crashed into the table. Scalding liquid and glass flew everywhere, Hack and Swift leapt back, and then I had two pairs of glowing, unsettling eyes locked on me.

"Knock it off, the both of you." I came around the counter and looked at them like misbehaving children, even putting my hands on my hips. "This is not happening in my house, damn it. We are venturing way too close to a realm of crazy that I am not fucking prepared to deal with today."

For a few agonizing heart beats they both stared at me and I felt like all the air had left the room and I was standing at ground zero, waiting for the ominous whistle of an impending nuclear strike.

Hack's eyes dimmed, the color bled back into Swift's and I took a shallow breath. The two turned to look at each other and gave a mutual nod, a slight dip of their chins.

"Hack, level with me, what the hell's going on? I have completely lost track of the number of times something's almost killed me today. There's no way this much crazy is coincidence." I felt more exhausted at that moment than I had all day.

"I'll be back." Swift spoke up and snagged his glasses off the table and put them on.

Without another word, he ducked out of the kitchen and was gone.

"Dangerous company you're keeping these days, boy," Hack said.

"He's my friend, he's helped me out a lot when things started getting rough around town." I shrugged, staring at the mess I'd made. I didn't know any fantastical methods for making coffee explosions disappear. I went into the pantry to retrieve a broom and rags. "You're deflecting. Why'd you come back?"

"Didn't you read that blasted email? It's the end of the damn world, boy." Hack dropped back into a chair. "Things that have been asleep are getting restless and their nightmares infect the world. The Sleeper's trying to wake up, Tommy, and its bat shit crazy servants are trying to bring it over to our side."

I had no idea what he was talking about but I didn't like the sound of any of it.

It did shed a light on the Libro Nihil's supposed appearance in town, though. A book reputed for containing the secrets of breaching the membrane between worlds would have every cult in the tri-county area on the hunt.

"What the hell is the Sleeper?" I looked up from cleaning.

"It's an Entropic, the worst possible kind of trouble; an avatar of one of the primeval forces, a cosmic god of chaos and ruin." It was Hack's deadpan delivery that did it for me. "The thing's been asleep for millennia. I don't know what got it stirring, but I felt it shift in its sleep all the way up in Washington. If it wakes up, that's it. Game over. Its followers will pull it into this world, and it'll snuff out every light in creation."

"Okay, stop. Seriously, you could've just said the world's going to end if we don't stop the colossal evil monster god." I finished cleaning up the coffee disaster and dropped down into one of the chairs. "And I would have accepted that, because that's the kind of day I'm having."

"I had to come back, Tommy. This is where the Sleeper's forces are gathering, they're after something they think will wake the bastard up and we can't let that happen."

That pretty much settled it.

The Sleeper's minions must have been looking for the Libro Nihil, and I would bet money Devlin knew that and that was why he put me on the book's trail.

It was time to go do something stupid, and if I botched it, it would end up with me dying a horrific death as well as the tragic and sudden demise of the entire universe.

"Time to go find us a book, then." I sighed.

7

"I don't care what he's doing, I need to speak with Devlin. Yes, Thomas Grey." I listened to the woman on the other end of the line chatter and frowned. "Pet wizard what? No, damn it. Listen, have him call me as soon as he can; it's about the end of the world. Kind of important."

Devlin was going to have to give up his source if I was going to stand a chance at finding the Libro Nihil before whatever mad cult was working for the Sleeper.

Swift showed back up not long after leaving with a sack of burgers. Whatever else he was, he was a decent guy. We sat down around the table to eat and plot out the next move.

“Any luck?” Swift passed around napkins.

“Devlin’s simpering minion said he’s busy,” I managed to mumble around a mouthful of charbroiled meat. “If he doesn’t call back soon, I’ll go pound on the door of the Red Manor.”

The Red Manor was Devlin’s castle, the seat of power from which he ruled over his tiny kingdom.

“You’re thinking Devlin knows where the book is?” Hack looked up from demolishing a burger.

“No, but I’m pretty damn sure he knows someone that does. What do you know about the book?”

He shrugged and reached into the bag, fishing out a handful of fries. “Probably about as much as you. When your great-granddaddy and I went after Abel Grannok, that sick son of a bitch was using a ritual from the damn thing to punch a hole through to the Other Side.”

“Grannok had the book?” Swift spoke up.

He took the words right out of my mouth.

“Supposedly, yeah. That horrible thing was the reason Henry left the old country. He chased that damn thing down his whole life, but died before he ever got his hands on it." Hack picked crumbs out of his beard and shrugged.

"How come I never knew that?" My brain was racing at the implications.

My great-grandfather had been a prolific writer, filling dozens of journals with stories of his adventures and run-ins with Others, all required reading during Hack's tenure as my mentor. But not a single one ever so much as hinted at the Libro Nihil, let alone Henry's suspicions of it being in the valley.

"Henry knew the book was somewhere around here. And somehow he heard tell Grannok had it, but we tore his farm apart and never found anything," Hack said.

"So the stupid book has been in Hanford this entire time. We're going to Grannok's farm; we have to try looking again." I stood up from the table and grabbed my bag from where it hung on the back of my chair.

For the first time all day I felt like I had a solid lead, or at least an idea of a direction to go in.

"Think you'll find anything?" Swift got up.

"Unless you got a better idea. I've worked with less." I

shouldered my bag and made to exit the kitchen.

"What about the cleaning lady?" Swift asked as I went.

I stopped in my tracks and hung my head. "Damn it."

I swerved down the hall to the living room. Rosa the cleaning lady was right where we left here, comatose and snoring on the couch. She was turning into a real thorn in my side and I didn't even know her. I couldn't leave here on my couch all day in a supernatural slumber, either.

I mean, I could, but it wouldn't be right.

I guess.

"I'm assuming just disappearing her is still off the table?" I glanced back at the other two.

Swift gave me a stern look and crossed his arms over his chest, and Hack raised an eyebrow.

I walked around the couch, inching forward, remembering the thrashing I received the last time Rosa was conscious. There was no good way to go about it, it was time to man up. Even though I knew no matter what I did it would end in tears, most likely mine. I went and took up a spot in front of the fireplace, putting a buffer of running room between Rosa and I should she awaken feeling punchy again.

"All right, do it. Wake her up, but both of you be ready just in case. She's stronger than she looks." I clutched at the strap of my bag, ready to use it as a shield

Swift nodded, expression grave. Hack watched the whole thing with an amused smile on his face. I flinched when Swift reached over from behind the couch to poke Rosa on the cheek. She twitched, her eyes fluttered, and she sat up and looked around.

Swift and Hack scurried to the other side of the room to hide by the china cabinets.

It was nice to know I wasn't the only coward in the room.

She saw the two of them as she looked around and gasped when she noticed Hack's eyes. She stood up with her hands curling into fists at her sides, and continued looking around the room until she landed on me.

"You." She said it like a curse, and pointed at me.

"Hola Rosa." I waved and managed a weak smile.

"Who are you? What do you want? How do you know my name?"

"You're wearing a nametag. Sorry about all the confusion. My name's Thomas." I was trying to speak slow and keep my voice calm; I didn't want to set her off.

"Are you going to molest me?"

My eyes went wide and I raised my hands. "Whoa. No, not at all. That's so not what's happening here. Do I look like, I mean, never mind." This was not going the way I planned. "Listen, do you remember anything from earlier?"

"Yeah I do, and I remember you and some crazy shit. You ain't natural. There's something wrong with you." She pointed at me again, and then swung around and pointed at Hack and Swift. "And them. What the hell's wrong with that guy's eyes?"

"He has a condition? We're looking into it. Rosa, we're not going to hurt you, cross my heart. But what you saw today? You're not going to tell anyone about that, are you?" I took a couple steps forward.

"And just who the hell would I tell that wouldn't think I was out of my damn mind? They would think I was crazy--I think I'm crazy." Rosa turned back to me, she took a step forward and I flinched back.

"Well, thank you. So, like, do you want a ride home, or a cab or something?"

"You can go to hell, brujo," Rosa spat. "You're a bunch of weird, evil putas."

I'm a lot of things, but I'm not evil. I am most definitely weird, there's no denying that. I'm not entirely sure what a puta is, though, but it didn't sound good. I let out a sigh and wrung my hands, gesturing to the hall.

"Whatever, lady," I said. "We were on our way out, anyways."

I walked out and the group fell in behind me. Once I had the door open and was outside Rosa brushed by without a word and stormed off, she got to the end of the drive, turned towards town and just kept moving, never even looking back.

I looked at Swift and Hack and shrugged, then went to get in the car.

"There's no way that's going to come back and bite you in the ass, boy," Hack said once we'd pulled away from the house.

"Nobody asked you, old man."

I ran through a quick check of my bag, making sure I

had everything I thought I was going to need and then some. I checked my cellphone a half dozen times in case Devlin called back, which he hadn't.

I hoped whatever business he was up to was more important than the impending destruction of Earth at the hands of an abstract cosmic entity.

It sounded stupid when you put it like that.

According to Hack's directions, what remained of Abel Grannok's farm was at the furthest reaches of the outskirts of Hanford, near the King's River. Swift drove, taking us past dairies and corn, acre after acre of orchard, and we took a cut-off from the freeway that ran alongside the dry riverbed and turned into a dirt track.

Swift slowed down on the bumpy road as it led into an acreage that had gone feral, what looked like gnarled walnut trees overtaken by valley oak and man-sized weeds. It was close to noon, the sun high in the sky, but under the trees, everything was shadows and watery light filtering through the leaves, the car kicking up dust to swim in the air like sad, brown ghosts.

"Close now, just a bit up the way." Hack leaned forward

from the backseat.

"Might as well pull over and get out," I said.

Swift complied, pulling the car off the dirt track and killing the engine. We got out and stood for a minute taking stock of the surroundings; nothing moved and the only sound was the freeway whispering in the distance.

"This is quaint." Swift nodded and looked around. "Like something out of a slasher flick."

"That's what I've got you and old laser eyes for. Who would be stupid enough to try something with two titans like you around?" I hefted my bag, heading down the path.

I hadn't gone far when I passed between a pair of rotted wooden gateposts driven into either side of the road.

"Place still feels wrong. That night, if your great-grandfather and I had shown up any later..." Hack kept his voice low as we cut through the shadows and dust.

"Do you mind? This is ominous enough without you yammering on." I trudged forward.

The trees spread out, growing further apart until we moved into a clearing, a space where the trees and brush created a rough ring through which the sky was again revealed and the sun beamed down. In its center sat the ruin of what used to be a farmhouse and barn, now little more than broken up slabs of concrete foundations and time-eaten timber. Debris was everywhere, trash and litter and detritus accumulated over decades.

"See anything with your magic eyes, Hack? Figured I'd ask." I looked around the clearing.

"You're hilarious, boy. I'll go root around by the barn, that's where Grannok was doing the ritual." The old man trundled off.

Swift was standing back and scanning the tree line, clenching and unclenching his hands, looking like he was itching for a fight.

I shifted through the spectrum and scanned around the clearing. I was getting a low-grade buzz of something Other, but chalked it up to residual energies from the horrible ritual years gone by and my current company. Looking at Swift's true form still put my teeth on edge so I kept him on my peripheral, and passing over Hack was bizarre.

All around his head hung a crackling blue aura like an

angry storm cloud. When things settled down, I was going to have to ask Hack about that piece of business. Looking around at the Other Side I could see a low mist creeping along the ground and the shadows were longer and deeper, like patches of empty void on the ground. Hanging in the air over where the barn used to stand was a rippling haze of light, like heat rising up off the street in summer.

The scar left over from Abel Grannok's attempt at tearing a hole in reality.

Looking around the old farmhouse itself, I could see shadows scuttling about in the mist, formless things moving around of their own volition. The likelihood of finding anything after all this time that would help my search for the book was slim to none, but I could do something to help with that.

Swift might be walking death and Hack a bona fide spell-slinger, but me, I found stuff. It's what I did. Secrets and lost things were my bread and butter, and finding them is how I paid the bills.

"Keep an eye out guys; I'm going to look upstream." I made my way over to the ruined slab of the farm.

I got to a nice wide spot of what used to be the farmhouse floor and kicked some things out of the way, clearing a space to work in. I fished around in my bag and pulled out what I was going to need: the stump of a black candle, a book of matches, and a couple sticks of chalk.

At the end of the day, magic is all about visualization and willpower, visualizing the effect you want and having the willpower to influence the forces you're working with.

I started by setting the candle and matches in the center of the space I had cleared, and began working out from there using the chalk to draw an ever widening spiral on the concrete, going counter-clockwise, backwards. Time is a river, relentless in its forward flow, branching off into little inlets where events left their mark on the stream. As I drew the spiral, I focused my will into it, concentrated on what events might have left their mark on time, in this space.

Messing with time isn't an exact science, and I could end up getting a glimpse of Grannok sitting down to a rump roast instead of anything useful. I just had to hope that something of enough impact occurred in this spot.

But given what I knew of Grannok and what had gone down here, I was willing to bet I would see something.

I finished drawing the spiral, holding tight to my focus, like a ball of pulsing light in my brain, and went to light the candle. When the wick flickered to life, I let go my hold on the magic, and the tiny flame glowed the bright, clear orange of a flame much larger. The spiral flared up, the mist and shadows began to dissolve. Wherever the light went, the shadows and mist fled, and ghost-like shapes appeared as the memory of the farmhouse that used to be, that lingered in the stream of time, began to take form.

A strong sense of disassociation always came with this kind of magic; it felt like watching a movie on strong acid, like you were inside of it.

It looked like I was standing in a half developed photograph; everything was blurry and grainy, kind of transparent and I could hear some kind of static like the wash of the sea in the distance, or the whisper of a thousand voices.

Shapes were beginning to resolve, forming out of the mists, and voices that began as tinny echoes far away grew clearer as I listened.

The voices were having an argument, the emotion made the words clearer, more distinct.

"You can't do it Abel, that book is evil. It's been nothing but a curse since you got it," one voice said, a woman.

Sounded like I was on the right path.

"You don't understand, Judith, it's shown me things. It has power, we could make that monster Desmond pay for what he did to us," the other voice, who I assumed to be Abel, fired back.

I frowned and chewed my lip. Desmond, as in Devlin Desmond? Curiouser and curiouser.

The two figures came into view, a man and a woman. The man, Abel, was rough and angry, his shape distorted and sharpened by a pall of dark energy that hung over him like a caul. Judith was faded, all washed out greys and whites, shrinking before Abel. She seemed terrified.

The scene rippled, shook, and Abel turned away from Judith to look straight at me, which was disconcerting as hell. He wasn't looking in my general direction but right at my face, which shouldn't have been possible. I was an impartial observer in a memory, but there he was, staring right at me.

And then he walked right up to me and shoved a finger in my chest.

"What do you think you're doing here?" Abel Grannok growled.

I was somewhere between freaked out and a stroke.

There was no conceivable way that Grannok should be able to see me. I wasn't even there. He wasn't even there. I was a ghost swimming in the time stream and watching the memories of reflections.

I was getting ready to pull the plug on the spell and run away screaming when I was overtaken by one of the most peculiar and disturbing sensations I've experienced in my entire life. It felt as if I was a cloud of smoke rising into the ether and disappearing, dispersing into nothing one atom at a time.

And as soon as it began, the sensation passed.

I stuttered and choked, my eyes began to water and I found myself staring at the back of what appeared to be a tragically deformed head, atop a body that was also quite the anatomical tragedy.

"The time has come, dirt farmer. You must act." The thing's voice was a rattling croak. "Screams echo in the spaces between the stars at the hunter's coming."

I froze.

Grannok wasn't looking at me, it was the pasty morlock he had been looking at, and that he wasn't on the verge of gibbering at the sight like I was, spoke volumes about the mad farmer's constitution.

The thing, whatever it was, was all wrong, twisted from head to toe, like a careless child tried to mold a man from putty and left it out to melt in the sun. It had the baked white eyes of a dead fish and naked except for a badly tanned loincloth; its skin bleached white and spotted here and there in patches of what looked like a crawling, yellow fungus. It had long, tapered ears and a wide bullfrog mouth filled with too many blunt, crushing teeth.

"You told me you'd take care of him, damn it," Grannok growled and his hands balled up into fists at his sides.

Abel towered over the hunched newcomer, but the man-thing took a step forward with a bestial, rumbling growl.

Poor Judith huddled up against the kitchen wall looking like she was trying to sink into it and disappear.

Seemed sensible given the circumstances.

"The hunter wields ancient powers, knows terrible truths." The thing twitched and moved about fitfully, scanning the room. "The ritual must be tonight or not at all."

"Can't be tonight, I'm missing a sacrifice. The book's damn specific about how many to offer up." Grannok had taken to pacing the small room, wringing his hands together.

"You have what you need." I shivered as the monster raised a long, pointed finger at the fading, shrinking form of Judith Grannok. "Do what you must, I will stall the hunter."

The scene began breaking up, the edges burning away becoming distorted. The last thing I saw before it all fell apart was Abel turning to loom over his wife and then the magic shattered.

And then I got plowed into by a gigantic feral pig.

It was one of the worst things I'd ever smelled, reeking of shit and rotting meat, and the damn thing had to have weighed half a ton; the air rushed out of my lungs, I howled in pain, and I heard Swift somewhere yell my name as I went down.

I did not want to die today. So far I'd survived beatings by a rabid bug-man and an angry Hispanic woman and wild swine were not about to be the death of me.

The impact raised hell on my already abused ribs and I caught one of the pig's hooves square in the hip, I screamed when I felt something pop and give way.

It was trying to gore me, drive me into the ground, so I did the only sensible thing I could think of and bit it, sunk my teeth into its neck. The taste of rancid meat made me retch but it squealed loud enough to almost burst my eardrums and flew off me.

I scrambled to my feet and almost collapsed when a lightning bolt of pain lanced through my hip and made me see stars. I clenched my jaw and hissed a breath out through my teeth as I took stock of the situation.

The pig that had railroaded me wasn't alone. There were six of the big stinking bastards, all them sick, putrid shades of purple and green with chunks of flesh missing, leaving swathes of guts and bone exposed.

Oh for crying out loud.

They were fucking zombie pigs.

I've seen everything.

Three of them were circling around Hack and his eyes were flashing while blue lightning arced around his hands, the old man seeming to be waiting for one of the pigs to make a move.

With my sight shifted, I saw that a subtle energy animated the pigs, what at first I thought was fur, black and insidious and crawling over their rotting flesh like a transparent horde of insects. And then a brilliant flash of light flew across my vision and I gasped.

Swift, terrible and glorious with his true form revealed, rushed straight at one of the pigs as it charged him, catching it and lifting the beast up over his head and then slamming it straight down into the ground where it exploded in a red cloud of gore. Chunks and pieces of rotten meat littered the ground around the fair sized crater the impact created.

I couldn't help but stare for a moment, mouth agape and eyes wide, and while my brain screeched at me in primitive horror at Swift, that he was a true herald of death, with his huge wings and strange, featureless form of pure white light, I could not help but find it, him, beautiful.

But there was trouble of my own to worry about as the pig that attacked me began circling back around, bringing a friend with it. The two zombie hogs approached from either side, intent on coming at my flanks to divide my attention, leaving me with little time for anything refined.

I was about to get flattened if I didn't come up with something. I saw the time-spiral nearby, abused but still flickering with lingering energy. I hurled my will at it and flung myself to the side as the charging pigs trampled onto the cement.

I hit the cement and tucked myself into the fetal position in case my trick failed but pain and death didn't come.

I poked my head up and looked over to see the two pigs frozen in mid-charge straight on top of the spiral as if someone had hit a cosmic pause button.

Thank all the gods and little fishes for small miracles.

I stood, wobbling a bit, and edged away, releasing my hold on the spell as I went and watched two confused pigs go charging past each other and off across the field as I breathed a quick sigh of relief.

I glanced around and saw Hack covered in ash, standing over the charred remains of three of the pigs, their blasted carcasses smoking on the ground in front of him, a vicious, tooth-filled grin on the old man's face.

"Hack," I shouted and pointed out at the running hogs.

He looked at me, and then to the pigs and threw a hand out as if he were pitching a baseball and his eyes flared up with blue fire, a bolt of lightning tearing out of his hand and smashing into the furthest pig, tossing its body up into the air.

Swift came hurtling out of the sky and smashed into the last remaining zombie pig, a blistering streak of white that burned my eyes. One went out and punched through dead flesh and he rode it to the ground as the thing squealed bloody murder, kicking and thrashing but Swift was relentless and landed blow after sledgehammer blow...

In the matter of a few heartbeats, there was nothing but twitching meat left and I couldn't help but stare at the spectacular amount of destruction caused between Hack and Swift. It was stunning. It took a moment, but I dragged my vision across the spectrum and back to normal while I caught my breath.

My heart thundered behind my ribs and I knew once the adrenaline wore off I would be in an all new and exciting world of pain.

Hack sidled over, giving one of the carcasses a kick as he did. "Doing okay, Tommy?"

"Wonderful, thanks. I can add 'undead swine almost killed me' to my list of achievements, now."

"Were you able to learn anything?" Swift walked up, wiping the filth and gore on his hands onto his pants. He was in need of getting hosed off.

I nodded. "Yeah, I did. Henry was right. The god damn Libro Nihil has been in the valley this whole time."

"What? How? We tore this place apart searching for it." Hack's eyes went wide and he looked to the ruins of the farmhouse and barn.

"Grannok had an ally." I shivered at the memory of the thing with the dead-fish eyes. "They must have gotten the book out while you were busy stopping the ritual."

Hack's brows knit up and he scowled.

Whatever or whoever Grannok's mysterious ally was they must have surfaced with the book again, causing all the recent madness I was now dealing with. Maybe the thing found someone new to pull off the ritual that failed all those years ago.

Whatever the case, I needed to find out what that freak was, and its connection to the book, because it was my only lead so far to find the stupid thing. It would seem I had no choice but to go bang down the door of the Red Manor and see Devlin. He was connected to it all; he was a part of it from the beginning, Abel Grannok himself said as much. Besides that, he kept detailed records of every single Other that had ever lived within his domain during his long and tawdry reign, like any paranoid but clever ruler should. I'd been trying for years to talk him into letting me see them.

"We got to move. We're going to see Devlin before this gets any crazier." I limped away.

"Boy I don't know if you noticed but we just got attacked by zombie pigs; this is about as crazy as it gets." I heard Hack grumble behind me.

We made it to Swift's car and back to the freeway, speeding along to town. I watched the countryside blur by, the quiet world outside the window and all the people that had no idea what kind of horror lurked in the world waiting to rain down hell and annihilation. Space gods of death, pasty-faced mutants, and evil books, I felt completely in over my head. I sighed and turned around in my seat to look back at Hack.

"Henry, he was a real deal magical badass, wasn't he?" I asked.

Hack's eyes went wide for a moment, and he nodded. "Yeah, he was. Most fearsome monster slayer I ever knew. That man's power could make the earth shake. Why?"

I shrugged and turned back around. "Grannok and his friend, they mentioned him, and you. They sounded scared shitless."

Hack chuckled, a cruel sound. I thought about my great-grandfather, and what I knew of him from his journals. And my grandfather, my own folks, too--all them bona fide monster hunters, magic makers and world shakers. And what was I? A bookworm with a penchant for sticking my nose where it wasn't welcome and getting my ass kicked. Every time I went looking for answers, digging for secrets, I was lucky I came out the other side alive.

I wondered what my family, were any of them still alive to see me, would think of me and what I'd done with my life and my power.

After a while, we cut off the freeway and hooked onto a road that carried us a few blocks north of Downtown, where the Bastille was, and into one of the oldest neighborhoods in the city. Some of the houses here were over a hundred years old, and the eclectic mix of architecture made for interesting scenery. Adobe haciendas stood next door to tall white Victorians and mansionettes, towering trees and manicured flower gardens like you saw in magazines dominating the yards. The neighborhood was one of the richest areas in town, home to old money and new money and some of the most prestigious families in Hanford so it made perfect sense that Devlin made his base in the area.

Swift slowed to a cruise as we got close to our destination as I scanned the houses. People roamed the sidewalks here and there, wearing expensive designer tracksuits and walking expensive designer dogs. Cars that were worth more than I made in a year parked in all the driveways. It was ridiculous.

“Might be best if I go in alone. Don’t know what Devlin will do if I come in with backup.” I frowned as we stopped in front of our destination “He can be kind of unpredictable sometimes, like if he feels threatened.”

“Why would he feel threatened?” Swift raised a brow over the rim of his sunglasses. He had wiped the majority of the gore off, but he still looked a fright.

“You exploded a pig. Wait here.” I got out of the car, leaving my bag inside, and turned around to lean into the window. “If I’m not back in ten minutes, feel free to tear the place down. Just make sure you give me an awesome eulogy.”

Swift killed the engine as I crossed the street and onto the winding cement path that led up to the sprawling expanse of the Red Manor.

The place was built along the same lines as the Bastille and shared many features with it, two daunting stories of red brick that looked more like an uprooted castle than a house, which was fitting for someone who fancied themselves the lord of the land. When it was first built a century ago, it was one of the first and most notorious mental hospitals in the state of California. And to add to the sinister aura, it specialized in child cases.

It shut down shortly after the Second World War when reports of the horrors that went on inside began to gain public attention. It stayed vacant for years, decades, until Devlin Desmond purchased it and turned it into his humble abode. He must have spent thousands on the lawn and flower arrangements alone, not to mention the rows of stained glass windows that surrounded the top and bottom stories.

I mounted a short series of steps and went up to a set of heavy oaken doors, banded with iron, the stained glass set into them stylized fancifully to resemble falling stars in white and blue and yellow. I knocked a few times and waited.

I was going to knock again when a shape passed behind

the glass and opened one of the doors. She wore a nurse's scrubs printed with a pattern of flowers, and she smelled like sunshine. I can't be certain, I was too enraptured by the way the light was turning her blonde hair golden, but I think a choir of angels began to sing somewhere.

I needed to start getting out of the house more often.

"Can I help you?" she asked.

"Oh god I hope so." I blinked and cleared my throat "I mean, I'm Thomas Grey. I'm here to see Mister Desmond."

"Mister Desmond? Oh, you're the man who called earlier." She began stepping back, pulling the door closed. "I'm sorry but he's very busy."

"See, that's unfortunate." I shoved my foot into the doorway to stop it from closing all the way. "Because there's an ancient primordial evil bent on cosmic annihilation, and I need Mister Desmond's help."

That all sounded a bit dramatic.

"Excuse me?" The lady was looking at me like she was trying to decide whether to call the police.

"Thomas, is that you?" Devlin's voice came from inside.

"My boy I was just about to call you. Sarah, do let him in."

The young nurse, Sarah, looked over her shoulder then back at me. She had bright, clear green eyes and was frowning as if she were still going to try shutting the door on me, which I didn't blame her for. With a small snort, she stepped back and let me in, moving out of the way. I could smell lemons and pine inside, and money. The whole place reeked of money. I had an urge to wipe my feet, and put my hands in my pockets.

"Sorry to barge in, Devlin, but things have taken an unexpected turn." I stepped in and looked around the foyer.

Tasteful, that's what the place was, but luxurious. Hardwood floors, rich rugs, oil paintings, those weird lamps with the stained glass shades. Devlin liked stained glass.

"Of course, of course." Devlin smiled and gestured at me, beckoning for me to follow. "Sarah, be a dear and get refreshments for our guest, we'll be in the study. Thomas, follow me."

Devlin headed for a winding, twisting staircase at the far end of the foyer, passing by a hallway and what appeared to be a large sitting room along the way. I made to follow him and caught Sarah giving me a hard look before she turned down one of the nearby hallways.

I'd like to believe she was enamored with my roguish good looks, but considering I'd recently gotten trampled by zombie pigs and was filthy, she was more likely wondering how long she had until she was going to have to call the cops.

I followed Devlin up to the second floor, feeling poorer with every step. The whole house was packed to bursting with priceless antiques and curios which made my own home look like a peddler's mall, and classical paintings hung in gilt frames on every wall. We went into a spacious office where the first thing I noticed was the far wall dominated by a massive series of windows that spread along the length of the room from floor to ceiling and gave an expansive view of the garden and sky out back.

And cleaning that gigantic wall of glass was a woman with a squeegee and dark hair pulled back into a tight bun. The hair on the back of my neck stood on end, the bottom dropped out of my stomach.

"Excuse me, Senorita Del Olmo, would you mind taking care of the silver downstairs now? I have company to deal with." Devlin moved into the room and made his way to a huge leather-backed throne behind a huge and impressive desk.

“Si Senor Desmond, no problem.” Rosa put her squeegee into a bucket on the floor beside her and began to turn. Her eyes locked onto me and went dark, furious, and her face twisted into a vicious mask. “Brujo.”

I waved. “Hi, Rosa.”

9

Rosa stood staring daggers at me, trembling, looking as if she wanted nothing more than to hurtle over Devlin's desk and see if she couldn't take a swing at me--which I hoped she wouldn't do because I was about at my limit for daily abuse.

I couldn't believe she was Devlin's cleaning lady. It was ridiculous enough to make me have to fight down a laugh that would have come out sounding more than a little unhinged. Devlin himself sat looking back and forth between Rosa and me with a curious look on his face.

"You two know each other?" He asked.

"Kind of." I nodded, not taking my eyes off Rosa in case she attacked.

I moved forward, keeping Devlin's desk between us. It looked like it would make a good barricade in a worst-case scenario.

"This pendejo's dangerous, Senor Desmond. You don't want him in your house," Rosa snarled and hiked her fists up as I moved.

"Thomas is my guest, Rosa. Mind your manners." Despite his calm tone, the 'or else' was well implied.

He stared at her and it shocked me to see that she stared right back, holding his gaze for a few breathless moments. And then without a word she gathered up her cleaning supplies and stormed out of the room.

Devlin sighed and watched her leave, sinking back in his chair. The monstrous thing made him look small, but did little to dampen the hard, clear look in his eyes, which he leveled at me once Rosa was out of the room. He nodded to one of the chairs in front of the desk, which was plain and looked much less expensive and comfortable as his own.

"And might I ask how you know our dear Miss Del Olmo?" He studied me, with little of the kind, light demeanor he had earlier in the morning.

"There was a scuffle at the Bastille today and she got caught in the crossfire. Being an idiot, I thought I would do a good deed and save her life." I fidgeted a bit under his stare, and shifted my own gaze out the picture windows behind him. " Which apparently pissed her off."

He nodded, drumming his fingers on top of his desk. "I did hear about that. The Caretaker was furious. Connected to the book, I'm guessing?"

"Yeah that's kind of why I'm here. What do you know about Abel Grannok?" I finally turned to look at Devlin.

"Abel Grannok was a dangerous psychotic tampering with forces far beyond his hope of comprehending," Devlin said it with no small amount of venom. "And he is now quite dead."

"Yeah but did you know him, personally?"

"No, not personally. I myself had only just come to the Valley, chasing the railroad. Times were...chaotic, back then." Devlin's eyes shifted away from me, looking at something distant.

Something of a sad, wistful smile crept around the corners of his mouth. “It was the Wild West, you see. Hanford itself was little more than farmers, rail workers, and the occasional outlaw.”

“Right. So then you had no idea he was in possession of the Libro Nihil before his capture?”

There was something he was avoiding, something he was keeping from me, there had to be. I’d heard the venom in Grannok’s voice, the ire of a man done wrong.

Devlin frowned and swung around to look back at me, eyes wide in genuine surprise. “He did?”

“Listen Devlin, I need you to level with me. The book is in Hanford, it has been all along. Grannok had an ally, someone who hid it away before anyone else could get it.” I leaned forward. “I need to know where you’ve been getting your information, how you knew about the book.”

He sat for some time, staring back at me, as if trying to decide what it was he was going to tell me. “If I must, then I will,” he said at last.

I half expected him to feed me another line about protecting his source’s secrecy or to devolve into platitudes but it looked like I was going to get a straight answer for a change, which was weird as hell.

That was when Sarah, the nurse, walked into the office bearing a couple of glasses and a pitcher of iced tea on a tray. It dawned on me that given the fact that Devlin was not the frail, eccentric octogenarian he played at being, he did not in actuality need a nurse. I frowned and watched as she set the tray on the desk, and noticed a slight charge to the air. I thought I felt it before, at the door, but was too busy getting distracted by choirs of angels and the way the sun turned her hair into molten gold.

I frowned as she left the room, taking the scent of sunshine with her, and leaving me wondering.

"She's a remarkable girl," Devlin said.

"She's certainly something." I turned back to Devlin. "So, as you were saying. Sorry but I really don't have all day, Devlin. Everything's falling apart."

Devlin frowned but that didn't stop me from launching into an attempt at describing the thing talking to Grannok I'd seen during the memory spell. All the while Devlin's frown grew heavier and he began to fidget, drumming his fingers along the edge of his desk, agitated and not a little disturbed.

"Deeper and deeper down the rabbit hole," he muttered when I finished talking. "Flesh-Thing. Stinking, twisted creature, it was here long before I arrived, lurking below the earth, venturing forth to seed havoc. To my knowledge, the wretched thing calls the sewers its home."

Mentioning the sewers brought unwelcome flashbacks of the Broken Circle and that abominable affair. But no matter how unpleasant, at least I'd gotten a lead. As usual, I could tell there were whole volumes Devlin wasn't telling me, the old bastard preferred his morsels of truth, but I still needed to pump him for answers on his mysterious informant, and time was wearing out.

I almost said something but never got the chance. Downstairs a door banged open, followed by voices raised in anger.

Devlin shot out of his seat in a flash, grabbing his cane as he went and marching to the door.

"Who dares?" he bellowed out into the hall.

For a time, a few minutes at least, I'd managed to fool myself into believing my visit to the Red Manor was going to be short, simple, and free of conflict, which only proved that I more than likely suffered from a mild concussion and no small amount of delusion. I cursed and stood, hurrying to follow after Devlin and jogging down the stairs. I caught up to him, and we made our way to the foyer to witness an absurd melee.

Rosa had Hack pinned to the floor on his stomach with a cleaning rag around his throat like a garrote. The old man's back bent in an unbelievable arch as she rode him, grinding him into the floor. His had turned a shade of blue reminiscent of his eyes as he gasped for air and floundered.

Swift, meanwhile, stood in the doorway covering his mouth with his hands and trying not to fall apart laughing, and Sarah stood to the side holding a cellphone in her hand, mouth agape as she no doubt tried to make sense of it all.

"I got him, Senor Desmond. This pendejo ain't going anywhere, you see I'll snap his evil neck," Rosa crowed, looked like she was about to, while Hack flopped and gasped, scrabbling at the rag.

"Desist at once." Devlin stamped his cane on the ground and it boomed through the room like a bell.

Everyone froze. Rosa let go of the rag and Hack hit the ground like a landed fish.

"What the hell, guys?" I looked from Hack to Swift.

Sarah still looked about ready to call the cops, and Rosa backed away from Hack but kept her eyes on him, while Swift worked to ride out the giggles and compose himself.

"We were waiting in the car like you said, but it had been a while." Swift shrugged. "Hack charged up the steps and kicked the door in. That's when the cleaning lady ambushed him. He never stood a chance."

"Just you wait." Hack wheezed from the ground, rolling onto his back. "I'll burn her alive."

"Hack Spencer you mad hillbilly, you'll do nothing of the sort. Stars above, you went and did it, didn't you?" Devlin moved forward, watching Hack.

Went and did what?

Sarah retreated back down the hall amid all the fuss and Rosa packed her cleaning supplies away while growling to herself in Spanish. Hack stood, rubbing at his neck as he met Devlin's eyes. Something went unsaid between them.

"Yeah, I did," Hack growled. "Starting to look kind of wore out your own self, Devlin."

Devlin gripped his cane and hefted it like a club, squeezing it so tight the wood creaked under the strain of inhuman strength. I took that as my cue and rushed over to push Hack towards the door while Swift slipped out to get the car started

"Hey, look at the time. Sorry about, well, everything. If you don't hear from me soon it's because I'm dead and the world will be ending shortly." I pulled the door shut behind me once we made it out.

We all piled into the car and Swift wasted no time pulling away from the curb and hurrying down the road.

I turned in my seat to look at Hack. "Mind enlightening me about what the hell all that was?"

"Thought we were going to find that book?" Hack stared out the window watching the road go by.

"Not until you tell me what that bit with you and Devlin was all about."

"We don't have time for this," Hack snapped.

"Oh hell no," I said. "Swift, stop the car."

Swift shrugged and pulled over to the side of the road, a car behind us laying on its horn as it passed. Hack turned to faced me, blue eyes flickering.

I took off my seat belt and climbed into the back seat. I ached in a dozen different places and it was no fun, but I did it. "Damn it, Hack, I know we got our issues, but I'm thinking at this point I kind of deserve to know what's up."

Hack snorted, blowing air out of his nose like a bull. He looked for a moment like he wanted to take a swing at me, but then the air went out of him and his shoulders sagged.

"I'm dying, Tommy," he said.

The words didn't quite register. They didn't make sense, like for a second he'd started speaking an alien language. Hack had lived longer than anyone I'd ever known. My grandpa used to tell me stories when I was a little boy, about when he was a little boy and in them Hack was already old. Time couldn't touch Hack, the thought of him dying, of not being there anymore, did not compute.

I shook my head, pushing the idea of him dying away. "What does that have to do with your crazy eyes?"

"Not too long after our falling out, well, my days of playing fast and loose with the laws of reality finally caught up with me." He shrugged, even managed to smile a little bit though it looked hollow. "So I did what I always do, I fought, and I found a way to beat it. Death, I mean. I beat it, with magic. By becoming one with my magic."

"What?" I felt lost.

"He became an Other," Swift chimed in front the front seat.

Realization crashed into me like a stinking undead pig and my jaw hit the floor.

The eyes, the way he went around flinging lightning like it was going out of style, the healing, it all added up. It was completely insane and the ramifications of it scared the living hell out of me, but it made a horrible kind of sense.

"No, I'm not a damned Other," Hack rumbled up at Swift and then looked back to me. "I'm still me, Tommy. But now I'm... more, too."

"How?" I had a million other questions but that seemed like the best place to start.

"Boy this is a conversation for another time. Unless I'm remembering wrong, we got a book to find and an Armageddon to stop," Hack said, and he was right.

"This is definitely not over, but yeah, we got to move." I considered getting back up in the front seat but decided it wasn't worth the effort. "So Devlin said Grannok's creepy pal lives in the sewers and goes by the name Flesh-Thing."

Hack and Swift made simultaneous noises of disgust as the car pulled back out onto the street and we got back on the move.

I looked from one to the other. "What now?"

"Haven't heard that name in years. Kind of hoped the ugly thing had died," Hack said.

Swift angled the car onto a main road and glanced up at the rearview mirror. "Death would've been too kind for that abomination."

I didn't have a clue what either of them were talking about, and didn't think it would do any good to ask them about it. But if Flesh-Thing or whatever the hell it was made its home in the sewers, I did know how to find it.

While the incident with the Broken Circle may have been a harrowing, disgusting nightmare, I did make the most interesting, and unlikely, of allies during that escapade, and he knew every stinking inch of Hanford's underground guts, not to mention commanded an army of millions.

"Swift, take us to the closest liquor store." I almost felt the urge to smile, but my face hurt when I tried.

"I'm not sure now's the best time to get drunk, Thomas," Swift said.

"Not for me. We're going to visit royalty, and it's only proper to bring gifts."

"Royalty? Ain't any royalty in Hanford, boy." Hack looked at me like I'd grown a second head.

"But there is, my friend." I managed a crooked, half-smile with a wince. "Uncle Satan, the one true King of the Roaches."

After convincing Hack and Swift that acquiring booze was integral to the continued existence of life as we knew it, I also convinced them into forking over whatever cash they had between them.

"So we just spent sixty bucks on liquor, and now you're going to go give it to some bum under the freeway?" Swift asked as we pulled away from the Stop-N-Rob and onto the road.

"Not just any bum, no." Hack shook his head. "The god damn king."

"Right, right." Swift nodded. "The king of the cockroaches."

I cradled the bottle in my lap and glared at the two of them. "Laugh it up, jerks," I grumbled. "Who do you think actually busted up the Broken Circle? Uncle Satan's the real deal."

When the Broken Circle had infiltrated Hanford's underground, hell-bent on turning the place into a debauched wasteland and freeing their abominable insect god, my only task had been to track the corruption to its source, to penetrate the unholy magics they'd been using to obscure their presence. Uncle Satan brought the thunder, him and his endless legion of many-legged minions. He was a local legend among the homeless and the destitute, who spoke about him more as if he were a god than royalty. I'd managed to figure he wasn't an Other--but I didn't quite think he qualified as a mage, either. Uncle Satan was unique.

I did know for an absolute fact, though, that reality and Uncle Satan were barely on speaking terms. The man was a loon.

We headed south out of Downtown, beyond the shops and suburbia, passing by the giant skeletons of abandoned factories and smoky dive bars. The roads were quiet enough, it being past noon on a weekday while normal folks were off slaving away in the mines, doing normal things, as proven by the parking lots and strip malls packed with cars, but even those grew more sporadic and derelict as we got closer to the looming hulk of the freeway.

It arched high above, a concrete and asphalt gateway splitting Hanford. Beyond it laid a town that had only just managed to crawl out of the Wild West, a city within a city where that scratched out a frontier existence. As soon as we slipped past the southern reach of the freeway's shadow, the property value plummeted and we entered a realm where even the police tread with caution, and for good reason: the human tribes dominated.

Southside proved that you didn't have to be inhuman to be a monster, and I worried more about the people than the Others. Life came cheap, crime and violence were easy. Which isn't to say the southern Others weren't a problem, they were. On the other side of the freeway dwelled the wild ones, the angry ones, the monstrous ones who had trouble fitting into a nice, neat human suit and playing along with polite society. Thankfully, they tended to stay off the streets during the day.

"Take a right up here and park it. The king's probably

giving a sermon at the tent city about now." I pointed to a dead field, an empty stretch of dust and dirt in the shadow of freeway where the detritus of Hanford's human population clung to a semblance of society.

While there were real tents strewn among the dwellings, for the most part, it was all salvaged cloth, timber and sheet metal thrown together into improvised lodgings. People in heaps of cast-off clothing milled about, some pushing carts laden with their entire lives.

Interesting fact few took the time to care about, but most of a city's homeless are wise to the ways of the Other Side out of a harsh necessity. The faceless and nameless were easy pickings for more predatory Others, and over time have developed an elaborate network of secrets and truths with which to defend themselves.

It explained why so many collected and carried odd trinkets and talismans, or exhibited bizarre, ritualized behaviors sometimes--other than the fact that many of were genuinely disturbed. The homeless, the vagrant, they knew the uncomfortable truth of the world: that we were not at the top of the food chain.

"This looks like a happening spot." Swift looked out at the tent-city and the folks milling about.

I stuffed the bottle of booze into my bag and headed for the field. "You'd be surprised, man."

There weren't even that many people out and about, most of them busy manning their posts around town, panhandling and scavenging, getting into who knew what. Swift and Hack followed close behind and the three of us got a wide berth and none too few suspicious looks. The invisible people weren't used to guests. I spotted a pack of people standing shoulder to shoulder in a circle by the overpass, in front of a large canvas tent, while a booming voice cut over the noise of the nearby traffic, coming from a giant figure in the center of the crowd.

"Can you not feel it? The trembling of the earth itself as a vile corruption twists about within its guts like a craven worm. Can you not hear the earth cry out its agony? That which has slept now rises, starved from its millennial slumber and it turns a mad, hungry eye on this world."

Uncle Satan stood seven feet tall if he was an inch and shared proportions with a grizzly bear. His dark piggy eyes gleamed behind a mass of wiry, filthy hair that created a ragged mane and gnarled beard where a great potato of a noise bulged. The beard moved, and the astute observer could see things crawling through its dark curls, brown backs catching flickers of light. Something resembling either a woolen, purple bathrobe or a sail draped around his frame and concealed a stupendous bulk and trailed along the ground at his feet while he paced. He stopped as we approached and turned to face my group, and every head around him turned as well as he spread his arms wide in welcome.

"Look, brothers and sisters, witness the Grey-Man, grave friend and deposer of false gods. What but grim tidings could bring him forth from his darksome abode? Grey-Man we implore you; share with us your words of doom." While Uncle Satan spoke, a bigger crowd formed, as everyone in the field came to see what the ruckus was about.

"The hell?" Hack muttered under his breath.

I shot a glare back at him, before stepping forward and bringing the brown-wrapped bottle out from my bag. The whole situation was ridiculous but it had been that kind of day. I cleared my throat, and lifted the bottle.

"Great king! True lord of the roaches, I come before you this day seeking your favor. You are a great and gracious king and I bring tribute, that you might be pleased."

Uncle Satan's eyes flashed upon the bottle and something hungry passed through the crowd; he nodded and made a brief gesture. One of the bag-people in the crowd darted forward and snatched the bottle out of my hands and it got passed over until it landed in the outstretched paw of Uncle Satan.

He stripped the bag off of it, turned it over in his hands and swirled it around, then held it up so that the afternoon sun could shine through it. He popped the cap off, upending the bottle into his mouth. The things in his beard writhed when some of the liquor splashed out while Uncle Satan took several long, gulping swallows.

"A good gift; the Grey-Man's gift is good!" He held the bottle out where anxious hands took it. "Name your favor, and we will do all within our power to aide you."

I had to concentrate on not laughing at how absurd it all was. Uncle Satan lived on a whole other level, but his power and resources were vast despite appearances.

"My companions and I seek a creature known as Flesh-Thing, who lives beneath the streets among the dark waters, a cancer eating at the heart of your kingdom."

The king stretched out his hand, and from his sleeve crawled out a titanic cockroach to stand tall and twitching its prodigious antennae in the center of Uncle Satan's palm. He held up to his face, near his lips, and whispered to it, and the bug bobbed up and down while its antennae scrawled odd, slow patterns in the air. They carried on like that for a couple minutes, the king and the cockroach, and then the roach disappeared into the shadow of Uncle Satan's sleeve as he turned to face me with a grave face.

"Indeed, Grey-Man," he spoke in low, close tones, "we do know this Flesh-Thing of which you speak. I hear the creature has begun again haunting the tunnels below our feet, whispering blasphemies in the dark."

"Do your legions know where Flesh-Thing hides?"

The king nodded and looked somewhere past me, raising his hand to point out to the south. "South, and down, always down, dear Grey-Man. I will dispatch an escort to show you the way." Hand still extended he turned again to face me, tracing a symbol in the air. I felt a subtle breath of power as he did. "Good hunting my friend, and doom to your quarry."

A noise rose from Uncle Satan as he raised his arms, a cacophony of clicks and rustling that grew to a din, then in a rush of sound cockroaches of all shapes and sizes flooded out from his beard and hair and robes, hundreds of them.

He shrank as they departed, diminishing as the swarm grew, swirling and darting about in a clattering dervish. The horde swelled to a writhing, man-sized cloud and then spilled onto the ground, before shooting off across the ground.

"Thank you." I made a short bow at the waist. "I'll see to it another bottle finds its way to you in the future, if there is a future."

Uncle Satan more resembled a gangling scarecrow than a bear, now, but he tipped his bushy head with a smile and turned to head back to his tent.

It was nice to have something finally work out and nothing had tried to kill me in almost an hour. Wanting to take advantage of my good fortune, I took off after the roaches at a brisk pace, Swift and Hack trailing behind. The swarm made its way across the field and cut across the street towards a main thoroughfare and onto another side street, ignorant of pedestrians and traffic as it cut an erratic, meandering path. The mind of a roach is anything but linear. We hustled to keep up and not get run over, and got more than a few honks and curses as we shot across the street.

The cockroaches led us to a sprawling complex, a distribution plant with a great big expanse of packing sheds and truck stalls, and a complex of raised mobile trailers acting as offices. No one was out in the yard and the lot itself was on the empty side, all surrounded by chain link fencing topped in gleaming rolls of razor wire. I skidded to a stop as the cockroaches crawled under the fence and kept going. There was a gate at the center on a rolling mechanism that I assumed someone inside would open when contacted by a truck driver bringing in a load.

Hack spat on the asphalt. "Don't suppose you got a key in that man-purse of yours?"

"Satchel," I fired back and clutched my bag. "Smart ass. I could probably hex it open, or hey maybe you could shoot some freaking laser beams out of your eyes."

While Hack and I teetered close to bantering, Swift stepped up, took the edge of the gate in his hands and gave it a hard shove. Sparks flew, metal groaned in tortured protest, and the gate went crashing back along its track.

I looked up. "Whatever."

Swift gave a curt bow and gestured through the now open gate. "Gentlemen."

The cockroaches were a shadow sliding along the ground, heading for an empty truck stall. We rushed to catch up after Swift jammed the gate back into place, and arrived to see the bugs had encircled what appeared to be a large drainage grate sunk into the center of a concrete pad. The grate itself appeared off-set, moved part way out of its hole.

"Down the rabbit hole we go, I guess." I glanced at Swift. "If you would be so kind."

He stooped, hoisted the grate up with one hand and tossed it off to the side where it landed with a jarring thud that cracked the concrete. The dank smell of mildew wafted up from the hole, and I could hear a faint rush of water down in the darkness. Hack came over and stuck his head down, eyes casting blue light over metal rungs that ran down the side of the shaft.

"Pretty handy." I snugged my bag on my shoulder. "Got any other fancy tricks, old man?"

"Like you wouldn't believe, boy."

I waved a hand at the hole. "Age before beauty."

Hack grumbled but got in and began making his way down. I watched his eyes, two shining orbs, as they sunk into the gloom, and then went in after him, leaving Swift to take up the rear. The smell kept getting worse, and the sound of water swelled to become a constant backdrop of static.

"Well," Hack hollered up, "it's definitely a sewer."

My feet hit bottom soon after and I stood there blinking, adjusting to the strange illumination cast by Hack's eyes. Wherever he looked two dim, blue spotlights went, and I saw we were standing on a narrow shelf extending over a fast running stream of water, inside of a massive pipe. I couldn't shake the feeling of being inside the city's guts, and the smell didn't help.

"What a shit hole," Swift said as he stepped off the ladder and looked around.

I got a candle out of my bag and dug around for matches. The light didn't stretch as far as Hack's blue beams but having an actual light made me feel better. The pipe we walked down stretched off in front of and behind us in a roughly north-south alignment until it faded off into darkness, with the water coming from the north so we made to follow its course. The walkway had a gentle incline to it that carried us further and further under the earth, further away from the sane, reasonable light of day. Part of my brain insisted going deeper into the sewers after Flesh-Thing would end in tragedy, and I tended to agree with it.

"This stinks." Hack trudged along, eyes roaming back and forth in front of us, illuminating the occasional spot where one intestinal tube of concrete intersected another, but always we went down. "Hope you know what you're doing."

"That makes two of us," I mumbled, trailing a hand along the rough, wet wall of the tunnel.

I decided it couldn't hurt--too much--to give a look across the Other Side, and stopped in my tracks when my vision slid across the spectrum. Glowing lines wormed their way along the walls to form a bizarre, twisting patchwork of alien glyphs and occult pictograms traced on every surface from concrete to pipe.

"Hey, stop," I called out and stepped closer to the wall to inspect the symbols.

Hack sidled over and his brow knit together, the light from his eyes putting a great swath of the wall and the writing on display.

"Bunch of gibberish," Hack said and scratched at his beard.

"Not gibberish." Swift stood behind me, scanning the tunnel up and down. His sunglasses were still on. "A very dead language, though, the last person to speak dust for thousands of years--supposedly."

"Supposedly? Seriously?" I turned to face him and Hack glared over as well. "Spill it, Swift."

"All right, but you're not going to like it." He took off his glasses as he turned to look at the wall. I watched as his eyes faded to empty white, and when he spoke, his voice swept over the rush of water and spread throughout the tunnel.

"Again the Sleeper will awaken and so begin anew the extinction harvest, the great dying, and the sundering of Creation."

11

"Fuck that." My voice bounced up and down the tunnel.

"We're doomed," Hack rasped.

"The rest is the same, a whole lot of apocalyptic jargon and emphasis that oblivion is awakening to consume Creation." Swift put his shades back on and shrugged, sticking his hands in his jacket pockets.

I began to wonder if I shouldn't have charged Devlin more than my usual rate. Maybe if I survived the whole debacle I'd retire from the professional snooping and look into getting a nice, quiet job at a library. See how the rest of the world did it for a change, what life would be like without the constant threat of supernatural extinction events and hostile, inhuman forces.

"Yeah, that settles it." I trudged back down the pipe after lighting a new candle. "We find Flesh-Thing, get the damn book, and you two annihilate anything that tries to stop us."

After walking for what felt like a small eternity, we came to the end of the tunnel, a large room where the pipe bottomed out and fed into a whirling pool of sewage in the center. The room itself was a rough box made of crumbling, moldering brick and concrete, it reeked of mildew and rot but the water pushed a cool breeze and moved the air enough to keep it from being suffocating and snuffed out my candle.

The room had a surreal air to it with the shimmering glyphs dancing along the walls and Hack's eyes washing it all in blue.

I stepped to the edge of the walkway and looked out over the whirlpool. "See anything?"

"Door, around the other side." Hack pointed. "Looks open."

He swiveled his head around as he spoke, revealing the

door in question. Heavy steel sunk into the brick of the wall, studded with rivets, with thick latches that sunk into the metal frame when closed. Part of me wondered what it would take to have something like it installed at my house. Like Hack said, it stood open, revealing only darkness on the other side.

Swift pushed forward and took the lead, moving around the walkway to the door. He poked his head in, pushed the door open, and disappeared inside.

Hack went in after him and lit up the situation before I followed. The small room I entered looked like it used to be a maintenance or storage closet, with rotted wooden shelves lining the walls stuffed with dusty tools and ancient boxes of unidentifiable supplies.

The rear wall, though, was not brick like the others. It was raw stone, the earth that the tunnels had carved through, and near the floor, a hole had been roughly hewn through the rock that I would have to stoop to get through and Swift would have to crouch.

“We followed a tunnel that led us, shocking and surprise, to another tunnel.” I gave Hack a shove towards the hole.

"Stick your head in there."

He smacked my hands and growled. "Stick your own damn head in there."

A noise came from the darkness beyond the hole, scraping, and rasping, labored breathing. Hack moved closer and looked down the tunnel, illuminating the outline of a figure as it dragged itself along the ground. It looked like a huge, pale worm inching itself forward with broken, erratic movements. A powerful stench rose from it, thick with rot and a hint of smoke.

It pulled itself into the light and I recognized the miserable creature.

Flesh-Thing.

"What happened to it?" Swift took off his sunglasses, frowning as he looked at the pitiable sight.

Its head wobbled around on an unsteady neck, and its eyes were gaping pits, the edges blackened, smoke still curling out from them. Flesh-Thing's mouth hung open, jaw almost unhinged, the thing screaming in inhuman pain though the only sound that came out was a strangled wheeze as it continued to drag itself closer.

It was horrible, and pathetic, but more than that, it was infuriating. Someone had beaten us to the pale bastard and ruined any chance we had of finding the Libro Nihil.

"Should just put the damn thing out of its misery." I approached Flesh-Thing, looking down at it, clenching my fists at my sides.

I began to make out hideous wounds across its hide as I got closer, angry scorch marks that almost looked like something had been trying to burn its way out.

I stood a few feet in front of it when its blind head swung up, straight at me, and the rasp that came from its mouth became a teakettle scream that echoed through the tunnel.

"It rises!"

I stumbled back, pain shot through my injured hip and I almost fell. When I looked over, I could see Flesh-Thing scrabbling across the dirt and trying to dig itself into the stone of the wall. Whatever it was going on about, the damn thing was terrified. Hack locked his eyes on it, framing it against the wall in blue light, and Swift went forward with a troubled look on his face to make a grab at it.

"The blood rises! The waking dream!" Flesh-Thing continued to scream even when Swift managed to wrestle it off the ground and into a chokehold. "The Neverborn dethroned!"

"I've about had it with this day." Something in my brain snapped and I saw red. My fist launched out and cracked Flesh-Thing square in the jaw.

It went limp, deflated and sagged in Swift's arms. I stumbled back, not thinking I'd hit it that hard--poor ugly bastard must have been in worse shape than I thought.

Then it lifted its head and swung around to level the charred pits where its eyes used to be at me.

"See," Flesh-Thing said in a pained whisper.

The word crashed into me and reality caved in on itself. Smoke and heat poured off of Flesh-Thing as if a fire had been lit inside the creature and Swift dropped it to the ground, backing away as it began to blacken and curl up on itself, filling the tunnel with a charnel reek. Meanwhile, I dropped to my knees and tried to hold my skull together while a flood of memories that weren't mine poured into my brain, visions and thoughts and feelings rushing through me.

I was in Flesh-Thing's head.

No, it was in mine. Everything that used to be Flesh-Thing crammed itself inside my brain. It had a name once, a real name, so long ago that the world had forgotten it existed. It, no his, he was a man once and his name was Knows-Secrets. The immeasurable weight of thousands and thousands of years dragged out behind him, a life that stretched back across a vast gulf of history. His memory, the things he knew and that whirled about in my mind, I could have disappeared in it all but for the bright, painful edge of something that hung over it all: a curse. It was vicious and brutal, and one that he had laid upon himself in some kind of penance for a grave sin. Once upon a time not only had Knows-Secrets been a man, he had also been a mage of great power.

Images washed across my vision and I saw a large group of people, familiar to me--to him. They were my friends and family, my tribe, and I led them to the valley that would be our new home, a paradise promised in whispers by the Sleeper, my god.

The images stuttered, flashed, and now my tribe, my family all lay at my feet with their bodies twisted and shattered, discarded like broken things. And I stood at the center of the massacre laughing and crying, screaming at the sky, tearing at myself and raging at what had happened, what I'd done. My people, their lives and their souls, devoured by the Sleeper, ripped away by lies and promises, but it was my fault.

No, not my fault, it was Knows-Secrets fault--but all he'd wanted was to see his family safe, and for that he succumbed to the madness and horror of the Sleeper's promises.

And so Knows-Secrets gathered all his power and created a curse, tying his own life force to the monstrous power of the Sleeper itself and granting him eternity to have his revenge. But the curse twisted the mind and body of Knows-Secrets and stole away his magic, for it took all his will to hold even a tenuous control over what he had done to himself and not succumb again to the Sleeper's influence.

The scene flashed again, zooming forward like an insane montage of time-lapsed video with years turning to decades and centuries, and then into millennia. All the sights and thoughts, the miserable spectacle of Knows-Secrets' long life crammed into my head.

And then it stopped, and I looked on a sight that I knew, something familiar: Abel Grannok's farm, as it once was when the madman still lived. It was night, the moon hidden behind a thick bank of clouds, and Grannok was outside speaking with Flesh-Thing, the creature that Knows-Secrets had become.

"You stole Devlin's book? He'll skin you alive," Grannok spoke in hushed tones, eyes wide.

"Not if you take its power for your own and destroy him. He took away your family's land, you could take it back." Knows-Secrets passed a small, cloth-wrapped bundle over to Grannok.

Grannok held the little package, running his hands over it. He looked like a starving man let into a free buffet. He scanned the clearing around his house, searching the shadows, as if someone were watching them, and then turned back to Flesh-Thing with grim determination on his face and an ugly gleam in his eyes.

"I'll do it."

Time shot forward again and I stood in the middle of an underground cavern. Light came from patches of mold and fungus that clung to the walls and cast a weak glow of sickly green light. In my, I mean, in Flesh-Thing's hands lay a small book. About the size of a pocket bible, its black leather cover simple and unadorned, tattered with age. The Libro Nihil itself, its appearance belied its true nature. As I turned it in my hands, ran my fingers along its cracked spine, a sound from across the chamber made me look up, and then the world erupted into pain and fire.

Burning, relentless heat slammed again and again into my back and head, my vision blackened and I screamed as the assault continued. The fire came from inside as well as without, and my screams went on forever.

"Don't worry, wretch, it'll be over with soon enough." A face, blurry, thrust into my vision but through the pain, it became clearer and as it did, a sickening dread sought to overwhelm the pain. "I'll be taking the book now."

And then Hack stood over me, shaking me like a rag doll. He yelled my name over and over. Screams filled the tunnel. It was me screaming, and from the raw, bloody feeling in my throat I must've been going on for a while. I choked and sobbed for breath, fire and darkness played in front of my eyes and

Knows-Secrets' memories still warred within my mind.

And the face of his attacker haunted me.

"Damn it Tommy, snap out of it," Hack hauled a hand back, about to slap me.

I shook my head and gulped in air, raising my hands to ward him off. He frowned, but helped haul me off the ground and onto my feet. The world spun, my skull felt as if it were made out of glass moments away from shattering.

"I'm all right," I rasped and winced.

"What happened?" Swift asked.

He still stood over the charred husk of the creature formerly known as Flesh-Thing, the mage that used to be Knows-Secrets. There was nothing left of it, nothing that resembled what it once was.

"Answers." I ground the heels of my hands into my eyes and tried to rein in my breathing, battened down my will and forced back the flood of memories. "Lots of answers. Knows... Flesh-Thing, the poor bastard, he wasn't the enemy. He was trying to find a way to put down the Sleeper for good and was going to use the Libro Nihil to do it--which he stole from Devlin, by the way."

Swift and Hack traded looks of shock and disbelief.

"Trust me, that's not even the most fucked up part. I know who beat us here, who took the book." Try as I might I couldn't think of any way around it. What Flesh-Thing had seen scared the hell out of me, and as for what it meant, I had no idea.

It made me want to start screaming all over again.

"Out with it, damn it. Who was it?" Hack came forward and shook me by the shoulder.

I winced and shoved him off.

"Henry," I whispered as his face rose up again in my mind. "Henry Grey."

12

"No, that had to have been a trick. It's not possible." Hack scowled, shaking his head, making the light in the tunnel go crazy. "Your great-granddad is dead, and has been for a long damn time.

"You don't say?" I snapped.

Memories that weren't mine still warred inside my skull, maddening chaos and not to a mention horrific headache. But I know what I saw. There were a dozen pictures of the man around my house, and I'd been hearing stories of his life since I was a child.

"Thomas, you're completely sure?" Swift spoke slowly, like he was talking someone away from a ledge.

I glared at him. If I didn't already know it would be like hitting a brick wall barehanded, I would've punched him. It wouldn't help anything, but it might make me feel better. I looked over at the charred remains of Flesh-Thing again and for a moment felt a twinge of sympathy. It spent thousands of years trying to make up for a single, terrible wrong. Thousands of years fighting a secret war only to have it all end in blazing agony.

"Yes, I am pretty god damn sure. But even if it was some Other bastard--no offense--wearing Henry's face, that doesn't change the fact that they still have the book." I started making my way out of the tunnel when a sudden random thought slammed into my grey matter. I spun and looked at Hack, "The blood."

"Say what?"

"It rises. Flesh-Thing kept going on about the blood and the hunter."

"Along with a lot of other madness, if I remember right. That thing was out of its damn mind, Tommy."

"Yeah but he was terrified. I'm pretty sure he knew Henry

was after him, after the book." Thoughts raced through my mind. Things were trying to grind into place. "When I saw it speaking to Grannok, it said the hunter was coming and the ritual had to be done. That was right before you and Henry showed up. Just now it was screaming about the blood rising, right after it got the living hell beaten out of it. You said Henry was a famous monster hunter, right, and had been chasing the book down for years."

"That makes a kind of sense," Swift said from somewhere back down the tunnel, "But then what's a Neverborn?"

"A what now?" I skidded to a stop.

"Neverborn, Flesh-Thing said something about a Neverborn."

"Ah. Yes, Neverborn." I nodded. "I have no clue."

Soon as I managed to put a few things together, something else had to come along and ruin it all, of course. One thing was for certain, I needed to get home and break out Henry's journals. He had been a prolific observer of the Others and compiled many volumes on all the different kinds he encountered over his long and illustrious career. The more I thought about it, the more I worked the thought over and rummaged around the corners of my memory palace, the more Neverborn stuck out. I'd seen it somewhere before, but I couldn't place it.

"Can we do all this ruminating somewhere that ain't a stinking sewer?" Hack stormed by me.

That punched me out of my reverie and we continued walking out of the tunnel. No time to follow our tracks back to where Uncle Satan's little helpers showed us in, I went for the first shaft of light beaming down from above, a short walk from the junction room where the sewage whirlpool roared, and I grabbed onto the rungs and began to climb.

At the top, an old-fashioned manhole cover sealed the shaft, thick and heavy and unmoving. I knew precisely how unmoving it was, because I only became aware of it when I slammed my head into the damn thing, too wrapped up in my head.

The pain reverberated through my abused skull and I shouted an explosive string of curses. Shafts of light beamed down from the ventilation holes in the manhole cover, and I held tight onto the rungs with one hand while I pressed my other up to the cover. It didn't budge. Not even a little bit.

"Need some help?" Swift called from below.

"Nope. I got this." I fixed my eyes on the cover.

Despite my body's aches and pains, I figured it would do me some good to flex my magical muscles and vent some frustration. I left my hand on the manhole cover, felt the cold metal. A bit of ugly evocation should do the trick, flash and fury like the chalk trick at the Bastille.

Magic, at its core, depended on two things: willpower and imagination. A basic understanding of it as a fundamental force, tools, and preparation are big helps, but in the end, it's all a matter of how much of your will you can throw at reality, and how far you want to bend it.

The manhole cover, for example, was a circular hunk of solid metal that probably weighed sixty or seventy pounds. On a good day, when I hadn't already had my ass kicked a few times, I'd have some trouble getting it to budge by main force alone. Exercise and I have never seen eye to eye; my strength was my mind. The way it stood, I could pound my head against the manhole cover all day and only get a concussion for my troubles. But, if I were to be a clever mage with an understanding of both magic and matter, well, that would change everything.

I kept my hand pressed flat on the manhole cover and began gathering my will, focusing on the currents of energy that underlies all creation, the universal force that magic taps into, and the spark of that force inside myself. I thought of the weight of the cover, the density of the metal, and I imagined it light as a feather. I sent out my will into the world, gave the cover a hard shove and it blew up into the air like it had gotten fired out of a cannon. Light flooded the little hole and I could see the sky again.

I laughed. One should never rely upon magic or allow it to become a crutch, but I'll be damned if it wasn't useful and awesome. I mean, it wasn't hurling lightning or turning chalk into comets or anything, but whatever.

"Way to go, boy. Now can you get your ass out of my face?" Hack grumbled.

"Yeah I'm going, hold your old ass horses."

I dragged myself out of the hole and stretched, wincing at the daylight and looking around. I sucked in a sharp breath.

We were not in a good place.

It was a narrow section of road, with trailers and run-down houses lining either side, little buildings that looked like decades had passed since they'd last seen any upkeep or a fresh coat of paint, their gardens wild snarls of weeds and yellowed grass when they weren't plots of dirt. It all made my house look like a mansion in comparison. Somewhere nearby a stereo was thudding with a ridiculous amount of bass, and I could see here and there low-riders with sparkling paintjobs and rims that cost more than most peoples' monthly mortgages, standing out in sharp and ridiculous contrast against the dilapidated homes.

I turned to tell Hack and Swift to hurry it the hell up when a door nearby banged open, and a flood of footsteps came out of a house across from where I stood.

I hesitated to look, but when I did, I saw around a dozen young Latino men were crowding out onto the street and they didn't look like they were coming to give us a neighborly welcome. They all wore red in an assortment of jerseys and button-ups, tank tops, and all had baggy jeans riding low on their hips.

But the most noticeable accessories of their varied ensembles were definitely the array of weaponry they were packing. They all carried something, some bats and pipes, some knives, and a few even had pistols out.

We'd gotten ourselves out of the sewers and ended up in the god damned Gardens.

While the majority of places south of the freeway were nowhere you wanted to be unless you absolutely had to, the tiny neighborhood referred to as the Gardens was a no-man's land; a warzone, a hotbed of gang activity in constant flux between the myriad rival tribes vying for control of it. The Hanford authorities washed their hands of it years ago, forsaking it to gang control and refusing to enter its limits unless a particularly bad conflict spilled out into surrounding areas.

Not the kind of neighborhood you took a leisurely stroll through.

"What the hell is this? You must be lost, gringo," the apparent leader said. He had a pencil-thin moustache and wore a bright red bandana around his head, and a large hand cannon stuck out of the waist of his jeans.

"Way to go Tommy. You landed us right in the middle of the damn ghetto," Hack said as he came up behind me.

"What the fuck's a matter with that puto's eyes?" The

leader said.

"He has a condition." I clutched at the strap of my bag. "And we were just on our way to the doctor, so if you gentlemen will excuse us, we'll be our way out of here."

The gangsters broke into a chorus of laughter.

"Oh, no man, no. You ain't going anywhere."

Behind me, I heard the creak of leather and looked back to see Swift squaring his shoulders and raising his fists. Hack was frowning, sparks flaring in his eyes. Across from us, some of the gangsters were beginning to look edgy, fingering weapons and the like. I did not have time to get dragged into a street brawl.

All the while, the stereo blasting the heavy bass beat kept getting closer and closer.

The leader stepped forward, hand on the handle of his gun, stopping a few feet in front of me. Any trace of laughter or mirth was gone from his face he gave me what I believe most referred to as a 'mad-dog' look. But that close, I could see the he was young, maybe in his twenties.

"You can't leave till you pay the toll, man. Or we beat it out of you. Your choice, puto." He said.

That damn word again.

I would bet a dollar it wasn't a compliment, considering the way he said it and the way Rosa had said it earlier. I don't think I liked that. Swift didn't either because before I could respond he shot in a blur in front of me, threw the young gang-banger into a vicious chokehold and had the guy's gun out and pressed up against his temple.

It got the reaction you'd pretty much expect it to. The street erupted into a lot of yelling and brandishing of weapons.

"Swift! What the hell man?" I hollered.

"Back up and I'll let him go soon as we're out of here." Swift edged away from the gangsters, taking the leader with him.

And if the ridiculous grin splitting his face were any sign, Hack approved of the plan.

I have the best friends.

From up the road came the source of the bass that had been throbbing in the background, now so loud it was vibrating through the soles of my shoes. It came from a lowered Cadillac that hopped and bounced to the beat on hydraulic suspension. It sped down the road and screeched to a halt within spitting distance from where our little altercation took place.

And Rosa jumped out of the car.

I groaned.

The guy Swift held, the leader, broke into a rapid fire shouting in Spanish. I couldn't make out much of it, most the Spanish I know comes from frequenting the taco trucks around town, but I did keep catching the word 'madre.' Mother? I think that about confirmed my recent suspicions of the day that some higher power got its jollies by screwing with my life.

Rosa stormed up and looked from the young bangers to my group and me, and if looks could kill, I would have been standing at ground zero of a nuclear strike.

"Stop!" Rosa shouted, her voice cutting over the other yelling like a knife and stopping everyone flat in their tracks. It was the most maternal command I'd ever heard.

Swift shoved the guy away from him, but kept the gun. The young gangster ran straight to Rosa, who gave him a fierce hug and then proceeded to slap him upside the back of his head. Behind them his friends snickered, until Rosa turned her nuclear stare on them. The whole pack of them turned tail and ran back into the house they came from.

"Hell of a lady," Hack murmured behind me with something of a grudging respect in his voice.

"What've I told you about trying to act gangster, Jesus? Get your scrawny ass inside," Rosa said to the young man, Jesus, who I assumed to be her son. He ducked his head, shooting me an evil look before he shuffled back inside after his friends.

"Hi Rosa. What a lovely surprise running into you." I tried to sound as pleasant as I could muster. "Again."

I'm not going to lie; when she came up to me, I flinched. I could feel the blow coming. Instead, she stopped inside striking distance and even though she was shorter than I she still managed somehow to look down on me. Despite all I'd been through, she scared me.

"What the hell is this, brujo? I want answers, and I want them now," she snarled, voice low.

"Yes ma'am." I nodded. I was too tired and in too much pain to argue. "But you're going to think I'm crazy."

"I already think you're loco, now get your white ass inside before some real gangsters shoot you."

13

Entering Rosa's house felt a lot like walking into the lion's own den, but it was damn cozy.

The furniture all looked like it came from a secondhand store but it was all in good repair and clean. The whole house appeared to be a study in the relationship between cleanliness and godliness; there wasn't a molecule of dust or dirt anywhere, on any surface. Hack, Swift, and I sat in the tiny living room of the house packed onto a worn leather sofa. I couldn't take my eyes off a painting of a doe-eyed saint hanging on the wall across from me, it had tracked us as we entered and I couldn't shake the feeling of it judging me.

Rosa's son, Jesus, had retreated to the back of the house with his friends; I could hear the low thud of a stereo playing and voices laughing, yelling somewhere behind the music. Rosa commanded us to stay on the couch before disappearing down a hallway. She came back out wearing a pair of sweat pants and a faded black and silver jersey. She'd let her hair down, and it spilled down to the middle of her back in salt and pepper waves. But even relaxed she remained a lioness, a deadly creature with smoldering eyes that locked onto me as she sat in a plush recliner across from us and folded her legs underneath herself.

"So, get talking brujo," she said.

I raised a hand and shook my head. "No, wait. What the hell is a brujo? And what's a puto? Starting to feel like you're making fun of me over here."

Hack and Swift snorted and laughed. I turned to look at them, but they both stared off in different directions.

"A little. Puto means bitch, brujo means witch," Rosa stated flatly.

Well I never. Bitch, serious? And witch? What is this, the

sixteenth century? Swift and Hack couldn't contain it anymore and both of them turned into a couple of giggling schoolgirls.

This is my life.

"Screw the both of you." I turned back to Rosa. . "Okay, so maybe one of those I can…kind of understand, but witch?"

"Which one don't you understand?" She perked an eyebrow.

"Witch."

"Which one?"

I sighed and ground the heels of my hands into my eyes. "Witch, why do you keep calling me a witch?"

"Why do you think? Throwing fire and crazy shit, I've seen a lot of things but I ain't ever seen anything like that. Walking furniture, crazy white fuckers with glowing eyes." Her face twisted into something like anguish as she spoke, and her hands flashed in the air. When she finished she looked exhausted.

Discovering the truth of the world, seeing the ugly behind its mask, can have many profound, and sometimes traumatic, effects. Some people can't handle it, the weight of realizing reality is infinitely bigger and scarier than they ever imagined. I mean, I grew up my entire life with knowledge of the weird wider world, family tradition and all. But for the vanilla folks out there, I couldn't imagine what it would be like to wake up one day and know that monsters are real, and they definitely want to eat you.

Not to mention the fact that they're fucking everywhere.

Rosa got a double dose of it; she got to see some of the crazier denizens of the Other Side and a mage at wit's end slinging volatile forces around. Despite the barely contained anger that hung around her like an aura, took it all rather well. She didn't seem about to crack and go running through the streets screaming, anyway.

"Yeah, not far off. But I kind of prefer the term mage, thank you, if we're going to be putting labels on things." I'd have to try and break it all down as simple as I could manage. I didn't want to risk provoking the wrath of the volatile cleaning lady. "But yes, I cast spells and harness arcane energies."

Rosa seemed to absorb that, folding her arms over her chest and narrowing her eyes.

"So you know magic?"

"More like I perceive and manipulate the underlying

forces of creation, bending them to my will and altering reality," I said matter-of-factly.

"Magic, asshole."

Hack snorted and choked down a laugh, I elbowed him in the ribs. People don't respect the finer subtleties of working with the powers of the universe. Anyone could dumb it down and call it magic, but it was so much bigger than that. Guys like Hack tend to take it for granted. They do quick and dirty magic and make it look easy, pulling from stores of power and knowledge of power built up over decades, or centuries, of practice. As mages go, I was still a young buck even though I'd seen most of three decades. Everything I did was kind of tame in comparison.

To put it plainly, I could bend reality, not tear it a new one.

"Right. Okay. Magic." I sighed.

"And what the hell was going on at the Bastille? Magic turf war?" Rosa asked.

"Not quite. There's something I'm trying to find before some bad, uh, people do." A clock hung on the wall and I flinched when I saw the time, just past three in the afternoon. We had to get moving. "If I can't, it's kind of the end of the world."

"Why don't you, I don't know, call the cops? The FBI?" Rosa asked like it made perfect sense.

As much as I'd love to call in the cavalry and inform them of the impending apocalypse, it would be an unprecedented disaster to do so. The Others have spent millennia hiding their existence, manipulating legends and mythology to cover their tracks, using disbelief and science against lowly mortals.

Humanity, while puny and relatively powerless, outnumbers the Others by a shocking margin, and would no doubt go to any lengths to exterminate every last remnant of the paranormal if it came to light that demons, monsters, aliens, vampires, and more dark and sundry entities existed and had been preying upon them since time immemorial.

It would get really bad, really fast.

Hack let out a snort and shot me a sidelong glance, old wounds, memories of an old argument. I frowned; now wasn't the time to go digging through the dirt.

"Not an option. And as much as I'd love to sit and chat about the finer details of the madhouse that is my life, I don't have the time." I rose off the couch and slung my bag over my shoulder. Hack and Swift took the hint and followed suit. "You know too much already. I'm probably putting you in danger just being here."

"So that's it? You tell me monsters are real, and now you're leaving? What if some more crazy shit happens?" Rosa stood, looking ready to start a fight.

"That's why I have to go. I'm already pretty sure someone's dogging our tracks, so the sooner we leave -" A loud pounding came from the front door. I flinched. "Expecting company?"

Jesus came sprinting down the hall and went for the door. Rosa looked like she was about to say something, but he already had the door open. There was a crack and the young man went flying back down the hall, bouncing off a wall and landing in a senseless heap.

Rosa screamed bloody murder at the sight, as two massive, burly looking figures wearing slouch hats and festively colored ponchos came through the door.

"Should've seen this coming," Hack spat and rose off the couch.

The two men had to stoop and turn sideways to squeeze themselves through the door. Both stood well seven feet tall, with wide shoulders and arms as thick as telephone poles that ended in shovel-sized hands. I could make out lantern jaws under the hats, and both sported blunt, tusk-like teeth jutting out from their mouths.

I stood slowly and rolled the kinks out of my shoulders. "Ogres? I hate my life," I muttered.

"But it's never boring." Swift moved forward, looking almost happy at the intrusion.

Then Rosa came flying out of left field, screeching one of her patented expletive-laden battle cries, brandishing a solid looking wooden footstool. She blew straight past me and slammed the stool into the face of the lead ogre. She might as well have been hitting a tank for all the good it did. The stool splintered and rebounded off the big lummox's head, knocking its hat in the air and revealing its beady little eyes. It grunted and sent Rosa sprawling with a casual backhand.

"You take the ugly one." Hack shook his head and raised his fists, little arcs of electricity crackling and racing up and down his arms.

“Which one’s the ugly one?” Swift laughed and launched himself at the lead ogre, a black and white flash that plowed into the lead ogre with a thunderous boom and drove it into a wall.

I made a dive behind the couch as Hack cut loose, launching twin streams of lightning at the remaining ogre. It squealed like a stuck pig but didn’t go down. From behind the couch, I could hear lots of yelling and crashing about as World War Three erupted in Rosa’s living room. This was terrible.

And then it got a lot worse.

Of course.

I poked my head out around the couch in time to see Jesus’s friends crowding down the hall to see what the commotion was, and then lose their collective shit when they saw the ogres. A couple of them went into attack-mode, the rest made a mad dash to turn and go back the way they’d come. This had the bonus of not only adding more yelling to the mix, but random bursts of gunfire as the panicking gangsters began unloading their guns.

“That escalated quickly,” I muttered.

One of the ogres roared and Swift went sailing over the

couch. Somewhere I could hear Rosa groaning, and Hack was yelling a prodigious number of creative profanities as he kept blasting like a mad artillery piece. I belly-crawled along the ground behind the couch and made my way to Rosa. She had gone down on the other side of the living room and lay on her back staring up at the ceiling with glassy eyes. An ugly lump had already begun to blossom on her cheek where the ogre nailed her.

"Rosa? Rosa are you okay?" I shook her shoulder.

"I'll kill it…hurt my boy…I'll kill it…" she chanted over and over.

She might have had a concussion. I started dragging her back to the relative safety behind the couch when a massive boom shook the house to its foundations and everything stopped.

I'd never been one for praying, but I was about to pick a deity and start. I poked my head up over the top of the couch and saw that one ogre was down, Hack crouching on its chest with his hands pressed against its face. There were smoking blast marks all over it, its head resembled a charcoal briquette.

The boom, though, had come from Swift. Debris still fell from where he and the ogre tore their way through a whole wall of the house, and the gangsters regained their senses long enough to make a break for it and bolt out the door.

That drew all the wrong kinds of attention. I could hear yelling rising up from outside, screeching tires, and behind it all the wail of a siren.

"Swift, knock it off, we have to get out of here." I stood and took in the chaos.

Rosa got up, leaning against a wall and surveying the damage to her home with a look of utter disbelief on her face. When her eyes landed on the crumpled body of Jesus, she pushed past pain and shock and went into some kind of super-mom mode. She vaulted over the couch, past the wreckage and over to him in the blink of an eye.

While she was trying to shout consciousness back into her son, I picked my way through the war zone of the living room. Swift picked himself up out of the tumbled down wall, splattered in thick, greyish ogre blood and dust. He looked like he'd been in a knock down drag out with a rampaging ogre--which was appropriate--but the bastard was grinning ear to ear.

"Was that entirely necessary?" I glared.

Swift looked from me back to the mess he'd created and started laughing. From what I could see of the ogre buried under the rubble looked like it had gotten beat to death by a wrecking ball.

"Boy, we'd better get. Crowd's gathering, law's on its way." Hack rushed up from behind.

"On it. Rosa, come on you have to go. We have to get out of here." I beckoned, glancing through the hole in the wall.

Rosa helped Jesus to his feet. He looked pretty battered but not bad, all things considered. He had the thousand-yard stare of a man recently concussed, a look I knew well.

"You think I'm going anywhere with you psychos?" she howled. "You just destroyed my house!"

"In our defense, they totally started it. And there's probably more on the way. Not to mention the cops. We don't want to be here when either of them shows up." I made for the door.

Hack and Swift hurried over to the Rosa's Cadillac.

Rosa mumbled something I didn't catch under her breath, but it sounded pained and exasperated, and started making her way to the door while supporting Jesus's weight. It would take forever to make an escape at this rate. I went over and got myself situated under Jesus's arm and between Rosa and myself we made it out the door. I saw Jesus's pistol lying in the rubble where Swift must have dropped it, and stopped long enough to scoop it up as we went and dropped it in my bag.

You never knew when a gigantic hand cannon would come in handy.

Swift either used his Angel of Death magic or hot-wired Rosa's low-rider, and had it pulled up in the front yard of the house with Hack riding shotgun scanning the area. A decent sized crowd of neighbors stood out on the street, trying to see what the destruction was all about, and I swore when I saw how many of them appeared armed.

I threw the back door of the car open when we got close and managed to maneuver myself, Jesus, and Rosa into the backseat. Swift didn't even wait till the door closed all the way to stomp on the gas pedal.

"Any idea what the hell that was all about?" Hack asked after we had gotten some distance between us and Rosa's house, making our way through the Gardens.

I had a pretty good feeling what Thing One and Thing Two had been there for, at least I kind of thought I did. We were being followed and most likely had been all damn day; first Bug-brain's assaults, Flesh-Thing getting handled, and now the ogres showing up out of the blue. And let us not forget about the fucking zombie pigs.

The Sleeper's agents were following us; Sleeper agents? They got the book away from Flesh-Thing, and sent in the bruisers to try and get me out of the picture so I wouldn't interfere with the Sleeper's minions trying to awaken it.

"Someone's following us; someone knows we're after the book."

"But who else even knows about the book?" Swift asked as he drove, taking us out of the Gardens and back onto a main road heading for town.

"The Sleeper and its merry monsters, obviously, and Devlin. He was the one who started this whole mess." I watched things pass by out the window while I tried to take a mental inventory. "And, if Flesh-Thing's memories are to be believed, my great-grandfather."

“Not possible. I was there when Henry died, Tommy. It ain’t possible,” Hack said.

“Have I mentioned you’re all crazy?” Rosa spoke up; Jesus was sleeping with his head on her shoulder.

“That’s not very helpful.” I frowned. “Well if it wasn’t Henry who beat the freak to death, it was someone that looked a whole hell of a lot like him. And why would someone do that? Swift, take us back to my place. There’s something there I have to check, and we should be safer. I’ll lock it down.”

“What about my car?” He glanced at me in the rear-view.

“Uncle Satan’s people won’t mess with it, it’ll be safe. We can pick it up after we’re done saving the world and not getting killed.”

Reacting to everything was getting old; I’d been getting bounced around and beaten up since I agreed to find the damned Libro Nihil. I wasn’t a fan of getting hounded by an enemy I knew nothing about.

Getting into the supernatural investigations business was a great way to pay the bills if you could live long enough to get paid, and a fantastic way to pad my burgeoning collection of weird crap, but one day it was most definitely going to catch up with me. We pulled up to my house with company already waiting out front.

14

Devlin stood next to a gleaming white Jaguar, tapping his fingers along the length of his cane and appearing to be in a state of distress I'd never seen before. It made my stomach clench up, seeing him frazzled like that. The being who had single-handedly subjugated all the disparate factions of Others in town and brought them to heel, who held the peace and now he looked moments away from breaking down.

Swift parked alongside the Jaguar and I helped Rosa get Jesus out, who managed to become coherent enough on the drive to stand on his own power.

Devlin rushed over as soon as he saw me. “Sarah’s gone.”

“Sarah the nurse?” Thinking of her made me think of sunshine, and as he came near, I could see Devlin’s cane appeared beaten up, cracked and burned.

“Shortly after you left the Sleeper’s thugs broke into my house, in broad daylight no less. I tried to fight them off but they overwhelmed me, and took the girl.” Devlin’s eyes smoldered a violent orange, his power bleeding across the Other Side, in a visceral reminder of his true nature.

I frowned and hurried to get everyone moving towards the house. “Get inside and tell me everything.”

I went through the business of unlocking the steel security door and held it open as my rag-tag collection of guests went in. They made their way to the living room as I shut the door behind me and secured the locks again. I checked over my shoulder to make sure everyone was down the hall, then turned back to the door and laid my palms on it.

I shifted my sight to the Other spectrum and the door and stones around it lit up with ephemeral sigils and formulae drawn over them.

Not only had Henry built the house to withstand nuclear attack, he also worked protective magics into the stones themselves, and over the years his descendants added their own wards and spells to the mix, including myself. I'd never tested the security system, but I'd always been glad to have it, and now it looked like it might come in handy. I pushed a fraction of my will into the door and felt a gentle vibration thrum through the house as the defenses activated.

In theory, the combined protections should stop the supernatural equivalent of a bombing, unless of course we were dealing with Henry Grey in which case he would shut them down without batting an eye.

Why would I even think that? I shuddered and slipped my vision back to normal before meandering along to the living room.

"You live in a dump, brujo," Rosa said as I entered.

She was going around the room pulling the white cloths off everything, revealing furniture and things that hadn't seen the light of day in years.

"Not all of us can afford a cleaning lady." I shrugged.

Jesus shuffled around looking at my father's collection of curiosities in the china cabinets, African ritual knives and fertility idols from the Amazon, the pickled fetus of a therianthrope and other things. Swift busied himself with getting a fire started in the fireplace, and Hack sat in one of the big recliners with his arms folded over his chest giving Devlin the stink-eye.

The laser stink-eye. The thought of which made me almost start convulsing with laughter, which I clamped down on before it could get loose.

"So, lay it on me Devlin. Let's see how much more screwed up this day can get." I collapsed into one of the newly uncovered chairs and sighed as its thick cushions swallowed me. I think it might have been magical.

Devlin stood at one of the boarded up windows, looking out the gaps between the wood. He turned to me with a furrowed brow and worked his hands over his cane, gripping it and worrying at it.

"It's as I said, Thomas," he said at last, "a pack of faceless men, servants of the Sleeper, burst into my home. While I struggled to fight them off, they slipped away with Sarah."

"Why didn't they kill you?" Rosa chimed in.

"Excuse me?" Devlin looked at Rosa like she'd started speaking gibberish.

"Not a bad question, actually." The magical recliner began working its spell on me, leaching away the adrenaline I'd been running on all day and giving my various aches and pains a chance to filter through. I groaned and sat up. "I've lost count of how many times the Sleeper's goons tried to kill me today. They sure as hell weren't pulling any punches."

"They tried, but I am not quite so easy to kill." Devlin squared his shoulders, eyes hardening. "But I was not their target; they went straight for Sarah and overwhelmed me with numbers."

"When Grannok had the book, women folk started going missing. He murdered the lot of them to fuel his ritual," Hack said, still staring at Devlin.

"You do not have to remind me," Devlin fired back.

Hack and Devlin stared at each other while a palpable tension grew between them.

"Okay, so, anyways. Devlin, what do you know about Henry Grey?" I asked. Devlin broke away from his staring contest with Hack and looked at me curiously.

"Your great-grandfather?" Devlin frowned.

"Yeah, him. I've got reason to believe he's involved in all this somehow."

"I never personally knew the man, but by all accounts he was a fearsome slayer of demons and dark gods, a hunter renowned the world over for his skill and power. Nothing I'm sure you didn't already know. But he's been dead for decades, how could he possibly be involved?"

I had the unsettling feeling that everyone knew more about my great-grandfather and family history than I did, and that there were a lot of details the dear departed man left out of his journals. Which reminded me I needed to dip away and take a look at those, if I could escape the clutches of the magical recliner; Henry's legacy and whatever the hell the Neverborn were, it all itched at my brain.

"That's exactly what I'd like to find out," I said as I stood, groaning at a series of pops from defiant joints.

Swift disappeared at some point during the conversation, but I could hear him rummaging around down the hall in the kitchen. Hack averted his gaze to now look anywhere but in Devlin's direction, and Rosa was keeping herself busy with fussing about the room cleaning things, which must have been a nervous habit. And at some point during all the rambling, Jesus wandered off into the depths of the house.

"Devlin, I'll see what I can do about Sarah. But I'm willing to bet if we find the book, we'll find her, too. You might as well hunker down here; it's the safest place I can think of. The rest of you can tuck in; I've got to get my thinking cap on." I said and received a round of wordless grumbling and shifting about as I made my way out of the room, "And try not to kill each other or anything silly."

I passed the kitchen on my way to the stairs and noticed Swift standing at the counter staring sadly at the heels of a loaf of bread and an empty jar of peanut butter.

"What kind of person has peanut butter and no jelly?" He sounded like his puppy just died.

"I'll go shopping first thing soon as we settle this mess. Until then, would you mind keeping an eye on Hack and Devlin? Something's up with those two."

He looked up and frowned. "Kind of like you and Hack?"

"I doubt it." I shrugged. "Anyways, I've got something to take care of, shouldn't be long." I left the kitchen before Swift had the chance to say anything else.

At some point, Hack and I were going to have to talk about the rift growing between us for the last few years. Granted, looking back on it all, I'd been acting like a young, greedy asshole. For real, what kind of self-respecting wizard goes and puts an ad in the yellow pages? Exposes himself like that? Who knows what kind of trouble I could have started? Trouble found me easy enough without me helping it out any.

I went straight for my computer once I got to my room. For years, I had been digitizing all the knowledge collected under my roof and in my brain, from ancient grimoires and texts on esoteric physics to the personal journals of my father, grandfather, and great-grandfather and any other shred of information about the stranger side of life.

You could call it a labor of love, but it felt more like an obsession which I guess is kind of the same thing. My goal was to create a definitive database, an encyclopedia of sorts. I shuddered to think what someone could do if they ever got their hands on half the things I'd stockpiled. Knowledge equated to power, sure, but in the wrong hands, that power could be dangerous.

I went through the motions, got into my database, and entered the word 'Neverborn.' It ran the search, estimating it could take a few minutes to complete as it went through the thousands and thousands of documents stored inside the computer.

While the computer hummed and worked, I opened up my bag and went through what I had left in it. Jesus's pistol lay gleaming on top; I pulled it out and looked at it. It weighed somewhere close to a ton. Years of watching movies had taught me everything I knew about guns, which amounted to knowing you pointed the dangerous end at things you wanted to die.

I laid it on my desk and checked the status of the search; still going, of course. I decided I needed to give myself an edge, something that would make me feel a little less worthless the next time I found myself in the middle of a battle royal, and my attention drifted back to the pistol.

I couldn't hit the broad side of a barn, but maybe I didn't have to.

Fun fact: years ago, when America and Russia were having it out over who could build the better bomb, the Russians came to the conclusion that they couldn't build a nuke with the precision or technical skill that the Americans were able to. So instead, they made the biggest damned bomb they could; adhering to the philosophy that if you make the explosion big enough, you didn't have to worry about aiming so much.

I swept a spot clear on my desk and laid the gun back down, pulling some chalk out. I began drawing a circle around the gun, to entrap the forces I would be willing into it. I needed a way to make sure if I shot at something, it would go down, kind of like the chalk comet, but on a different scale. I worked magics of inertia, velocity, and destruction into the circle, and infused it with some of the burning power of the cosmos itself. The working swirled about in my head as I drew around the gun, building and growing, adding layer upon layer.

When I felt like I had poured enough of myself and my will into it, my head swimming with the effort, I reached forward, put my hand flat on the gun and breathed out. I released my will, my hold on the brimming forces, and pushed them down into the circle and into the gun. The air smelled like ozone and a ripple went through reality as if through a pond, and little stars burst and flickered in front of my eyes.

The gun felt warm under my hand, and a quick glance across the Other Side showed it glowed with a faint, inner light and streaks of angry red energy limned the barrel. I couldn't tell how well the enchantment worked without firing it off, I could only hope it wouldn't blow up in my face when I did use it. I looked over at my computer to see that the search finally completed, likely it'd done for a while. Magic tended to distort time. On the screen I saw that one result had come up, one entry among thousands in reference to my query. And just as I'd thought the reference came from one of my great-grandfather's journals. I opened the file the search directed me to and scanned through it.

Son of a bitch.

Years ago, Henry had met a curious creature that came to town following the railroads, claiming that it came from the distant future. It said it belonged to a race of beings that travelled back in time, a race that in Henry's time did not yet exist.

You see, they'd never been born.

The Neverborn.

Henry recorded the name of the creature and I cursed as I read it, though it didn't surprise me in the least. Recent events being what they were, it only settled some speculations I'd already been having. I shut down my computer, put on a semi-clean hoodie from a pile on the floor and slung my bag back over my shoulder, placing the gun inside before making my way back downstairs.

I could hear raised voices as I approached, when I came around the corner into the living room Hack and Devlin were standing and shouting with Swift standing between them to keep the two from lunging at each other.

"You knew the whole damn time! I ought to blast you to smithereens you sorry parasite," Hack growled, a storm cloud of energy growing around him.

"What would you have me do, you cantankerous red-neck? Appear weak before the wolves?" Devlin fired back, his cane raised like a war club and burning orange.

In the time I'd been away, Rosa somehow managed to pry some of the boards away from the windows, and late afternoon light filtered into the room. She now sat on the couch, along with Jesus who reappeared at some point, watching the argument go back and forth like a tennis match.

"How about not lie to the boy?" Hack snarled.

Try as he might to appear serious, I could see Swift trying hard to contain a smile. Despite the gravity of the situation and that the two could reduce my house to a smoldering ruin, it did look like a round of geriatric fisticuffs was about to go down.

"Not lie to the boy about what?" I asked finally.

They stopped when I spoke and walked into the room, still glaring daggers at each other, or lasers in Hack's case.

"Everything Tommy, every damn thing. He knew Flesh-Thing had the book the whole time," Hack said, flinging an accusing finger at Devlin.

"And for the pathetic creature's own safety, I kept it secret. It was safer in its labyrinth than it ever was with me." Devlin said, lowering his cane.

"Your super mysterious informant, it was Flesh-Thing all along wasn't it?" Another piece of the bigger picture crashed into place "What the hell did you hire me for?"

Devlin's shoulders sunk, he let out a sigh like it was a breath he'd been holding in for way too long. He gave an almost plaintive look to Hack before turning to face me.

"When it first stole the book from me I was furious. Years of searching for a way to destroy one of the Entropics all for nothing, until I cornered Flesh-Thing some years after the incident at Grannok's farm--"

"Figures, Senor Desmond's a freak too," Rosa muttered from the couch.

Devlin pretended not to notice the comment and continued.

"He needed to find a mage powerful enough to enact the ritual, only those blessed by Creation to harness its forces can wield the book, you see. And while Grannok certainly had his flaws, he made up for it with raw power." Devlin turned to cast a sidelong glare at Hack again. "The Sleeper would've been destroyed, all those years ago, if it weren't for two hot-headed hunters ruining everything."

"How were we supposed to know?" Hack threw up his arms.

Devlin scowled at Hack and crossed his arms sternly over his chest.

"I let Flesh-Thing keep the book; as I said, it was safer down in his labyrinths. I had my hands full trying to calm the chaos that arose after Grannok, and over the years, I lost contact with Flesh-Thing. I assumed since this mud ball kept spinning he still had the book and all was well, until the Sleeper stirred.

I knew I had to contact him and get the book, but I couldn't be certain the Sleeper's agents hadn't already gotten to him. Someone or something was following me, which meant whomever I contracted to find the book would also be in danger. I used you Thomas, I'm so sorry. When you took the case, it began to become more and more clear who it was leading the Sleeper's minions. The only other person who ever knew I possessed that book."

I shuddered. The one piece of the puzzle I kept hoping wouldn't be true, that wouldn't line up, fell into place. But since my whole life was one big nightmare study into the nature of Murphy's Law, I should have known better.

"Yeah, the only person who knew that you're a Neverborn," I said quietly, barely able to admit it to myself. "My great-grandfather."

15

"How many times I got to tell you? It can't be Henry, damn it. I watched him die." Hack shook his head.

After the revelation, Hack shot up out of the chair, eyes spitting sparks, fists and jaw clenched. I wish I could be half as certain about anything; that kind of outrage is good for a person. Rosa and Jesus had retreated from the living room after declaring it too full of crazy for normal people.

A sentiment I agreed whole-heartedly with.

"Did you see the body?" Swift spoke up for the first time since we arrived, spooking everyone.

I didn't remember him coming into the room from the kitchen, and he went so long in silence, standing and watching everyone, I kind of forgot about him.

"Excuse me?" Hack turned on Swift.

"Henry's body. When he died, did you see it?" Swift asked as he contemplated the peanut butter sandwich in his hand.

Staggering logic from our friendly neighborhood celestial being.

I'd seen enough bad horror movies and read enough comics to know you never count someone dead until you've seen the body. Come to think of it, I'd never even seen a grave for Henry. It had happened long before my dad's time, and my grandfather said the battle that took Henry's life blasted the countryside so bad that the official town record blamed it all on a rogue asteroid.

"He's right, Hack," I said, and shuffled back a step when Hack leveled his unblinking blue stare at me.

Devlin smiled as he watched the exchange, tapping his cane absently on the ground. "How did you walk away from that fight unscathed, Hack? I'd heard the psychophage left no survivors."

"Henry, he saved me," Hack said. He looked so tired, and collapsed back into the recliner. "He sacrificed himself to banish that horror and buy me time to escape."

"That settles it, then." I wanted to set something on fire, or hop on the next flight to Alaska. "My great-grandfather is back from the dead and working for an ancient, colossal god of ruin."

Rosa took that moment to poke her head into the living room. "Hey brujo, there's someone here for you."

"Excuse me?"

"Some guy at the door says he's looking for you," she said with a shrug and disappeared again.

I poked my head out of the living room and Rosa making her way down the halls, collecting a pile of tarps, cleaning as she went. That was kind of neat, if not a little invasive. Unexpected visitors in the middle of a crisis were not so neat. I looked back into the living room. Swift stood at one of the boarded up windows, looking out between the slats.

"I don't see a car," he said.

I fidgeted, shifting from foot to foot and edging towards

the hall. "Do you see anything?"

"Older guy, black hat and black coat, he's by himself--maybe a Jehovah's Witness?" Swift glanced back with a shrug.

Hack shook his head and Devlin looked like a cat with its hackles up, claws out and spoiling for trouble. I got the feeling whoever waited outside did not come bearing good news or glad tidings. I could open the door and get blown to pieces, or worse.

My teeth began humming, and it felt like a small army of ants were marching along the backs of my eyes. Something lurked across the Other Side, dreadfully powerful.

I might have a small advantage or two though. For one, the wards all over the house still worked, otherwise the stranger would already be inside. I also had the now enchanted pistol in my bag, and figured it might be a great time to test out my latest dabbling in enchanted firearms. I hefted the gun out, and did my best to square my shoulders and straighten my spine as I made my way down the hall.

This turned out to be more of an ordeal than I imagined, with every step I had to push against the prodigious force of the stranger as if making my way down a wind tunnel. I ground my teeth together and planted one foot in front of the other, trying to keep my shoulders straight and my head up. I'd never been one for bravery in the face of overwhelming odds. I felt much more inclined to go running back up to my room and hide under the bed.

I banished that thought as best I could and determined not to succumb to baser urges. Not far off, I saw the front door stood ajar. With a deep breath, I knocked it open the rest of the way, letting the pistol hang loose in my hand at my side.

The man standing outside looked wrought from porcelain and shadow, his skin dead white in contrast to a long coat and hat so black they sucked in light. His eyes were a solid, empty black, and when he leveled them at me, I could feel the weight of his gaze like a physical thing. He stood close to my height and we shared a similar build but menace and an unearthly power poured off him in waves.

"Thomas Grey?" he asked in a low bass rumble tinted with a curious accent.

And I tried to speak, I tried to respond.

Instead, I found myself nodding dumbly, and found it hard to hold onto the gun, it felt like it weighed a thousand pounds. I started shaking.

The guy smiled, thin lips peeling back from perfect, straight white teeth. It reminded me of something I read about monkeys a long time ago. A monkey's smile is a threat, a warning.

"You're not exactly what I was expecting. I'm Henry. Henry Grey. I believe I have something you're interested in." The smile kept growing.

For a brief moment, in my mind's eye, I pictured myself raising up the pistol and howling nonsense. My hand twitched and I shuddered. Henry continued with his unsettling smile.

"That's so weird," I managed to mumbled, "That was my great-grandfather's name, too. You kind of look like him, you know. But that would be really weird, seeing as he's dead and all."

"I have no time for foolishness, Thomas. I came to make you an offer." The smile never faltered, he clasped his hands in front of him and inclined his head.

"It couldn't possibly be an offer I can't refuse, could it?" I'm clever. I forced a shaky smile back at him.

In my mind another visual flashed, this time coming like a kick in the chest and staggering me. I saw myself with the pistol held up to my head, screaming, pulling the trigger.

And then I saw...nothing.

I started to get angry. Angrier, more than in the tunnels with Flesh-Thing, angrier than I'd been in a long time. I am not a fan of having my head messed with. I gathered my will together, pulling at the energy invested in my home and all around me, and I lifted the pistol, but not to my head. I pointed it straight at Henry's face.

"Knock off the mind-fuck. Get off my land before I put a bullet in your face." Between the mental assault and the strain of pulling down so much energy, I fought to get out every word, speaking through clenched teeth.

Henry chuckled, a low growl that promised evil things worse than the threat of his smile. "The blood hasn't watered down that much, I see." Henry took a half-step back and the overwhelming pressure pouring off him faded away. "I want you with me when I become God."

That's definitely an offer you don't get every day.

"Join me and you can have the Libro Nihil, and with it power over the life and death of every being on this planet." He swept his arms out wide as if to encompass the world.

"And all it'll cost is my soul, right? What kind of asshole do you think I am?" I'd stopped shaking as my anger grew. The energy I collected fed off it, boiling and writhing inside me, aching to be set free. "Fuck you, Henry."

I pulled the trigger, and set the energy free.

Fire and thunder exploded from the barrel of the gun, a great blazing cloud of it billowing out to consume Henry. The force of it blew me back and threw me down the hall to go slamming into a bookshelf. It hurt, and I screamed in pain at the impact as books toppled off the shelves in an avalanche on top of me.

The enchantment definitely worked.

Hack, Swift, and the others came running down the hallway while I picked myself off the ground. It looked like they were talking but all I could hear was a sharp ringing in my ears.

Hack came skidding to a stop and turned to face the door, his mouth hanging open. Devlin stopped right behind him as a lance of solid, inky darkness came streaming down the hall. It took him full in the chest and tore him off his feet, not stopping until it slammed into the ceiling, pinning him there.

I could see him screaming even though I couldn't hear it, flailing and writhing at the thing that pierced him. Smoking spots rose on his body as the vicious darkness burned away at his insides.

Rosa and Jesus bolted back down the hall. Swift went flying across my vision and slammed into Hack, still standing dumbstruck, and tackled him out of the way of three more of the black spears. My hearing began to come back, enough that I could out the rising sounds of chaos. I made it to my feet and turned to look down the hall to the door, where Henry stood.

He walked through the door without setting off a single ward, which made sense considering he'd made most of them. The blast from the pistol hadn't harmed him at all, either.

He raised a hand and around it hung an aura of festering, roiling darkness. And his smile was gone. "You are a weak, stupid little worm, Thomas Grey. You could have been a god."

"That's not nice," I mumbled, head pounding.

I was going to die, along with everyone else bottlenecked in the hallway. The pall of darkness around Henry's hand grew, throbbing as he prepared another strike.

Hack pushed his way forward, stepping between Henry and me.

"Go on Tommy, out the back. Me and Henry got some catching up to do," Hack growled. He patted me on the shoulder and turned to face Henry.

My great-grandfather let out a nerve-wracking laugh. "My dearest friend how you've changed. But you can't save him; you can't save any of them."

Hack didn't waste any more time on words. The last thing I saw was Hack shooting down the hall like a bolt of lightning, his whole body flaring up with blue and white light before he slammed into Henry and blew him out the door.

I caught a look at Devlin, fallen to the ground with his eyes wide and empty, his body smoking and beginning to disintegrate, before Swift dragged me down the hall and made his way to the kitchen. Rosa and Jesus were there, hiding under the dining table.

"Thought you said your place was safe brujo, what the fuck happened there?" Rosa snapped as she crawled out.

"That was crazy!" Jesus shouted, looking at everything with wide, jittery eyes.

"No time, got to run." Swift went to the kitchen door that led out to the back of the house.

I felt numb as I followed, and ended up getting pushed along by Rosa and Jesus. There were noises coming from the front, from the battle between Hack and Henry, thunder and howling wind as if the end of the world had come down in a maelstrom.

"Where's Senor Desmond?" Rosa asked.

I shook my head. "Gone."

It surprised me how much that upset me. Devlin, monarch and warden of Hanford's Others, snuffed out like nothing. For more years than I'd been around, Devlin kept the peace and kept the more dangerous Others in check. He also tended to be my primary source of income, hiring me on for research and information.

All of a sudden, it looked like I'd be trying to stop the end of the world pro bono. There would be no more checks coming in.

That also made me sad.

Rosa let out a venomous string of Spanish. I finally noticed that I still clutched onto the pistol with a death-grip, and eased it into my bag. I wanted to say something to Swift about facilitating our escape when he came tearing around the back of the house in Rosa's car, kicking up a cloud of dust as he skidded to a stop.

We wasted no time packing in and he tore off across the barren field around my home, making for the street. The sounds of Hack and Henry's fight had been a horrible soundtrack in the background, but as the low-rider fishtailed onto the road, the noises stopped.

I stuck my head out the window and looked back at my home. Hack and Henry were gone but the front of the house looked as if it had gotten caught in an artillery strike. I slipped over to look at the Other Side but saw nothing but a simmering pall of colorless energy hanging around the yard.

"Where to?" Swift asked. "Thomas, where are we going?"

I had no idea. Devlin got murdered right in front my

eyes and Hack more than likely would be dead soon, too, if he wasn't already. Henry possessed the Libro Nihil and stood unopposed in his ambitions.

I could be certain of only one thing at that point, as I hung my pounding head out the window.

We were well and truly fucked.

16

After my house disappeared into the distance and we made it into the city proper, surrounded by the mad rush of five o'clock traffic, I found myself entrenched in a sense of dread.

In the rush of it, of the normal folk so blissful and ignorant of the madness and horror around them, it would be easy to get lost. I'd spent many quiet hours, late at night alone in my room, dreaming of a so-called normal life, something menial and tedious, something banal and safe.

I longed to be brave enough to wish for a life where I never worried about looming apocalypses or evil bogeymen trying to murder me and devour my soul. Knowledge of the Other Side could damn you for life, or kill you and annihilate everything you held dear. Rosa could attest to that.

A brutal, heavy silence hung inside the car, everyone lost in their thoughts, trying to hang on to the quiet and not speak. I started to, a couple times, but kept my mouth shut. Rosa sat in the back with her arms folded over her chest, looking out the window at the darkening sky. For once she didn't look furious, or pissed off, or like she wanted to hit something. She looked tired. Jesus sat next to her with a glazed over look in his eye, more than likely trying to run everything he'd seen through his head and make sense of it without going mad.

Swift had sunk into a distant silence as he chauffeured us around town aimlessly, cruising along the road and turning onto streets with no particular destination in mind. From the passenger seat, as I watched him, I could see his eyes darting about behind his glasses, scanning everything.

I turned to look out the window, to watch the traffic and the city slide by. I knew what would happen next.

I managed to piece almost the whole puzzle together.

The pieces I didn't have were easy enough to guess, looking back on it all. At some point in his quest for the book, Henry became a thrall of the Sleeper and faked his death to scheme and grow his power.

When the stars aligned or however he managed to determine the timing, he flushed out all the competition and used me like a fucking idiot to get him exactly what he wanted: the Libro Nihil. He took Sarah, a convenient victim and sacrifice to help power the ritual he'd use to pull the Sleeper over from its prison on the Other Side.

I couldn't help but wonder if maybe I shouldn't have taken the bastard up on his offer.

God of a wasted ruin is still better than dead.

It might have been the handful of head wounds talking, but why did Henry make the offer in the first place? I couldn't help him much in a fight and my power paled in comparison to his. Magic that guys like Henry or Hack spit out like nothing left me floored with a migraine. Did he feel some bizarre sense of familial propriety to me? That would be ludicrous, I'd never met Henry in my life, and he didn't strike me as a particularly sentimental kind of guy.

Unless, of course and it should be obvious, it had nothing at all to do with family. Because I'd been so busy trying to not get killed that I completely overlooked one tiny, but possibly significant fact.

"He thinks I can stop him." I sat up and winced at the movement.

"Oh yeah, you got him scared good." Rosa laughed.

"Hush, you. It makes sense," I snapped. "Why else would he try to get me to join him? He could've come in guns blazing."

"He did the whole guns blazing thing, though," Swift added helpfully.

"Only after I threw his offer back in his face."

"You mean after you shot him in the face," Jesus said under his breath.

"You guys are a bunch of fucking comedians. I'm being serious here."

"Okay, I'll bite," Swift said as he eased up to a stoplight. "If he thinks you can stop him, why not just kill you? Why bother trying to recruit you?"

"The same reason Flesh-Thing needed to find a mage. The same reason Devlin needed to find a mage. Because he can't do the ritual," I said, quite satisfied with myself.

"But he's like the super bad-ass version of you, brujo," Rosa said. "Grande brujo."

"I don't think he's a mage anymore. I think he's become something like Hack is." I thought about it and frowned. "Was, I mean. Like Hack was."

"You think he's become an Other?" Swift asked.

I nodded, letting the thoughts meander about in my brain and come together. It made as much sense as anything else. Like Hack, who merged his energy with the greater flow of Creation, Henry merged with the Sleeper. Maybe becoming some kind of twisted avatar of the Sleeper itself, which meant he couldn't manipulate the Libro Nihil anymore because he wasn't in truth a mage anymore.

Henry had become something Other.

Since I turned him down, that meant he needed to get another mage to enact the ritual to bring over the Sleeper, and us magical types weren't exactly heavy on the ground. So where would he find another mage?

"Hey, Swift, did you notice anything out of the ordinary about Sarah?"

"Devlin's nurse?" He glanced over at me. "Super pretty, completely out of your league."

Rosa snorted from the back seat. I ignored her and continued.

"Besides that. You ever wonder why Devlin needed a nurse to begin with?"

He shrugged. "I'm going to hazard a guess and say because she's fun to look at?"

"Yes!" I punched at the dashboard in triumph, caught up in my own train of thought. "I mean no. No, that's not it at all, you jerk. Devlin needed a mage, too. Damn it, I can't know for sure without looking at her from the Other Side, but I'd bet my teeth she's a latent mage."

If Henry wanted sacrifices, he could have his pick. I'm sure if I felt like breaking into the local police database I'd see few missing women that'd cropped up recently. But why would he attack Devlin, after he'd already gotten the book, if there wasn't something else he needed? Because he needed a back-up plan if I shot him down.

That's why Sarah was at Devlin's to begin with, the crafty old bastard had been grooming her to awaken to her dormant potential. Unfortunately, it all felt kind of secondary to the fact that an innocent woman was in the hands of a monster and in need of rescue.

It kind of sucked for her that I would be the one doing the rescuing.

"So what's your brilliant plan this time, brujo?" Rosa asked, accompanied by a round of chuckles from Jesus.

"We're going to start with getting Swift's car back, then you two are going to get the hell out of Dodge till this is all over," I said, Swift nodded and took the nearest turn to lead us back to his car.

"What if that creep comes back?" Jesus asked, pushing his head forward between the seats. The fear in his eyes made him look awful young.

By all rights, Henry shouldn't have any interest in Rosa and her son once they were away from me, in theory at least. Except maybe as hostages to use against me in the inevitable chance I showed up to stop him.

That kind of pessimism didn't help anything.

"You guys will be fine." I tried to sound sincere.

I caught a look from Rosa in the rearview mirror; she didn't look like she believed me but must have found some pity in her heart and decided not to voice it, most likely for Jesus's sake.

I spent the rest of the ride double checking the gear in my bag. The pistol still had some rounds in it, and I flicked over to the Other spectrum for a second to make sure the enchantment on it still lingered. Not as bright as before, but the barrel still crackled with a vicious light. It would have to be good enough. All my other things looked to still be intact and in order. When we got to where Swift had parked his car, he got out and went running over to it like a long lost lover. I swear he caressed the steering wheel when he slid in. Jesus and Rosa moved into the front seats of her car, Rosa getting behind the wheel. I made it halfway to Swift's, when I turned around and called back to her.

"Listen, I'm kind of sorry about all the weird shit that's happened today."

"I take it back, brujo. You're not evil, just crazy. And stupid," Rosa said, revving the engine of the low-rider and peeling away before I could respond.

I stood for a moment and watched her speed away into the distance. She was probably right on both counts; I'd have to be crazy and stupid to think I could take on Henry and have a chance at stopping him. But at the moment, I didn't have any other options.

Swift honked and I flipped him off as I turned and walked to his car.

"You really think they'll be safe?" Swift asked after I'd gotten into the car.

"Safety is pretty relative at this point." I put on my seatbelt and chuckled. "We should get moving."

Swift gunned the engine and let the tires squeal, slinging the car out into the street and aiming for the freeway entrance. Super dramatic and flashy thing to do, bordering on the obnoxious. But I let him have his fun.

I tried not to let him see how much I enjoyed it.

"You know what the funny part is?" I asked after we'd

gone past the city proper and crept up on farmland and dairies.

"That you're massively out-gunned and stand little to no chance of surviving?" He grinned and flicked on the headlights.

"That's not funny at all." I looked across the car at him. "Level with me, you're really some kind of angel?"

I tried to see what road he pulled onto but missed it when he started into a full-blown, honest to goodness laugh session. Complete with slapping the steering wheel. He pulled off to the side of the road and parked the car, until the laughter subsided into a series of fading chuckles.

I backed into the door, trying to hide or make myself smaller. When over the laughter ended, Swift turned slowly to face me, a strange smile on his face. He moved a hand from the wheel and took his glasses off, the mirth disappearing from his face, eyes blank and white.

"There's so much more to it than that, Thomas," he said, his voice calm. "And if you survive the night, I'll be happy to tell you everything."

"That was fucked up, man."

The barest hint of a smile pulled up the corners of Swift's

mouth as he cranked the car back into drive and slid out onto the road, slipping his shades back on.

We were out in the country, a few miles outside the city limits. Farmland and dairies spread out around us as far as the eye could see, the sun beginning to make its way down and setting off all the weird colors that only the questionable valley sky could turn. The raging pessimist in me felt it a good time to take it all in, get one last long look. Swift could be right; it might well be my last sunset. Stopping Henry seemed impossible.

Shooting him in the face with a magical hand cannon hadn't achieved a damn thing.

"You have no idea what to do, do you?" Swift asked.

"Correct, sir." I shrugged. "Want to just go grab a bite and wait for the end of the world?"

"Thomas I don't care if he is your great-grandfather, if you let Henry destroy the world, I will kick your ass."

It meant a lot to have such supportive friends in my life.

But I also felt a bit like a selfish jerk, thinking about it all, entertaining the slightest urge to succumb to defeat before the fight even started, or cave to Henry's offer. Hard to believe so much horror, pain, and death because of a stupid little book. The memory of it, Flesh-Thing's memory of it, still lingered in my mind. Such a tiny, insignificant object. The memory of it...

"Son of a bitch, pull over the car!" I scrabbled to open my bag and began tossing its contents out.

"What'd you just call me?" Swift swung around.

"Pull over the damn car!" I shot him what must have looked like a mad man's glare and in my sudden zeal dumped my whole bag out in my lap.

Swift looked like he wanted to say something, but complied and ended up pulling into a little service station off the side of the freeway. I'd begun cackling at some point, pawing at the door until it popped open and I went spilling out of the car in a wave of papers, books, chalk and various assorted oddities.

"Nothing to see here folks, just a psychotic break. Carry on." Swift got out of the car and hazarded a benign wave at the scattering of folks in the parking lot. "Thomas what the hell are you doing?"

"Books man, beautiful, stupid books," I sprung on him, shoving my copy of The Golden Bough in his face. "I have books too."

"Okay, it's all right. Slow it down, man. You're going to have to break it down for me. Sanely. People are starting to look nervous." He put his hands on my shoulders and spoke slowly, calmly.

People never understand the true nature of genius, damn it.

I took a step away from him and drew in a few deep breaths, shoving my brain into order. A plan began formulating in my mind, but it would require equal parts heavy duty screwing with reality, and an absurd amount of dumb luck. I would more than likely end up dying a horrible death.

"Fuck with my head, Henry, I'll fuck with yours." I laughed and held up my book.

17

Swift was busy inside the gas station, trying to convince the manager that I wasn't a threat to myself or others and to not call the authorities.

I sat out in the middle of the parking lot, scrawling out a hideously complex circle ringed with runic script and shot through by gibberish. I would need to trap a dangerous amount of energy, and focus it into a carefully crafted illusion. Something good enough to pull a fast one on my great-grandfather, and a lot of it relied on memories from an ancient, half-insane mutant shaman that were tattooed onto my grey matter.

What could go wrong?

Flesh-Thing possessed the Libro Nihil for decades; he knew every page of it, every crease and tear. Which meant, in theory, I did too. Kind of. Most of what got shoved in my head was a gigantic, jumbled mess and a lot of it had already begun to fade. But if I could hone in on those last moments before Henry attacked Flesh-Thing, I could use it.

"I told the manager you're my autistic step-brother and we're on our way to Disneyland. I promised him you're harmless," Swift said as he walked up, carrying an armload of junk food and a fountain drink. "I also spent about a hundred dollars on non-sense."

"Why do you hate me?" I looked up at him after putting what I hoped would be the finishing touches on the circle. I knelt in the center of it, with my copy of the Bough in front of me; the circle with its accompanying scribbles sprawled out a few feet all around me.

"Just hurry it up. The natives are growing restless." Swift looked around, shuffling his hoard of snacks in his arms.

"You hurry it up," I grumbled.

Unless I botched this, which could happen, it should work--in theory. I could worry about the whole confronting my great-grandfather when I got to it. Dwelling on it now would only make me scared. More scared. And scared people tended to do stupid things.

Things like perform heinously elaborate magic while looking like a complete lunatic in the middle of a gas station parking lot.

The conditions were about as good as I could hope for, despite a few bewildered looks and whispered comments from passers-by, and the whispered rush of traffic from the freeway. The sun already began its dip towards the horizon, dragging the peculiar colors of the valley twilight and heralding the evening's chill.

The wind had a soft bite to it that carried the aroma of cow shit along with the cold. I tried to empty myself of everything, pain, fear, anxiety, and absorb the world around me. I opened up that hidden part of myself that held a spark of Creation, fanning it to life like stoking a flame. I focused on that energy, gathering it, collecting it, holding onto it.

I figured I had gathered enough of the stuff once my temples began to throb; now I needed something to tether it all to, to help give it shape. With my mind emptied of all but intent, I filled it with the memories of Flesh-Thing that still lingered, on the Libro Nihil. On every last little detail of it, the tattered black leather cover, the curious weight that belied its size, the lethal aura that emanated from it. With my eyes closed, I reached forward and gathered my copy of the Bough in my hands and lifted it, slowly, opening my eyes and slipping my vision across the spectrum as I did.

All around me the circle and symbols rippled with light, a haze shimmered in the air with the colors of an oil slick inside, surrounding me, and all the energy I had gathered. In my hands I held a pulsing, book-shaped object of light.

So far so good, now it was a matter of fixing the magic into the shape I wanted. I bore down on the image of the Libro Nihil in my mind, on the energy inside and around me, and I stood. I felt like a semi-truck rested on my shoulders, the force pressing on me from all sides, and my breath came in labored gasps by the time I managed to stand straight. I stepped forward and broke the circle, releasing my hold on everything.

Instead of shredding me apart, the magic roared through me and filled my ears with static. It ended as quickly as it began and left me wheezing. All my old pains and worries came flooding back to fill the void the magic left while I worked to catch my breath, but it seemed the spell worked.

In my shaking hands, instead of my familiar Golden Bough I held a little black book, no bigger than a pocket bible, and with my vision still shifted I could see angry black veins of darksome energy throbbing across it.

"I'll be damned, you did it. You really...Thomas, are you okay?" Swift came forward, shining in his true form, reaching out to steady me.

"What?" I wobbled on unsteady legs and winced at the glare coming off him.

I switched back across spectrums. I had something in my eyes, something wet, and my head pounded with a profound pain that threatened to drown out all my body's other aches. I clutched at the book with one arm, and wiped at my face with my other. The sleeve of my sweater came away wet and red with what looked a lot like blood. My blood, I could feel it running down my face and staining my vision red.

"For fuck's sake man, sit down." Swift herded me back towards the car and got the door open in time for me to collapse into the passenger seat.

I caught a look at myself in the rearview mirror, and I laughed.

It made my head hurt worse, but I laughed. One of my eyes was completely shot through with red, blood vessels burst, and a steady stream of bloody tears was streaking down my face. More dripped out of my nose, and got into my mouth when I laughed. I coughed on it, gagged.

It's was a possibility I'd over extended myself and tried messing with more magic than I could reasonably handle, and I might've had some kind of aneurysm. That figured. I couldn't help but laugh at it.

I heard Swift listing off expletives under his breath as he fired up the GTO and tore out of the parking lot of the gas station. I looked down at the book in my lap which I still clutched tight in my hands. I did it; I pulled it off despite almost killing myself.

For all practical points and purposes, the book I held looked like a perfect replica of the Libro Nihil. Perfect enough to fool any of the ten to twelve sense; a palpable aura of power hung around it. It was just a giant ruse, it didn't have any of the power of the real thing, but it would work for my purposes.

"We have to get to Grannok's farm," I said when I'd finally found my voice again.

"One undead livestock related near-death experience wasn't enough?" Swift glanced over and frowned.

"It's where Henry will be, it makes the most sense. The border between this and the Other Side has already been weakened there, I saw the scar from the last ritual."

"And you're sure you can handle Henry?"

"Nope." I laughed, and winced. "But there isn't a lot of choice, is there?"

Swift grunted in the affirmative and took the next exit that would lead us to Grannok's farm. The sun had crept below the horizon while I worked my magic, and if I were the death obsessed servant of a colossal cosmic entity in the market for some doomsday, I'd be gearing up to get my evil on.

Henry more than likely already started laying the groundwork for the ritual, and who knew what he had done to Sarah. If she were awakening to her powers, and in the clutches of my great-grandfather, she was probably scared out of her mind. I didn't care to think about what he might do to get her to complete the ritual.

Scenery became a blur as Swift sped down the road, foot heavy on the throttle. It all melted together, the dull throbbing in my head, the throaty growl of the car's engine. For the first time all entire day, my brain wasn't spinning a million miles an hour with a barrage of thoughts and anxieties. Likely due to a world of pain and a fatigue so deep it settled into my bones. I was on empty, sucking fumes. I hoped I could hold it together long enough to at least make a show of trying to stop Henry.

Instead of focusing on anything useful, I spent the majority of the trip thinking of all the creative ways my great-grandfather would annihilate me.

It's always better to prepare for those things in the event they should happen, it lessens the trauma.

"We're getting close, you ready?" Swift knocked me out

of my reverie, probably for the best, as he swung the car onto the familiar dirt path that led to Grannok's farm.

"Sure." I dragged myself into an upright position. "You can let me out here."

Swift stomped on the brake and I caught myself before I could smack my face into the dashboard. The false Libro Nihil went tumbling onto the floorboards and I scrambled to pick it up then shot a glare at Swift.

"What the fuck was that?" I hollered.

"Drop you off? I know you might be brain damaged, but are you stupid too? Henry will tear you apart if you go in by yourself." Swift sounded outraged, skirting as close to anger as I'd ever seen him.

"I have to go in alone." I turned away from him. "So that I can get Henry's attention, so you can rain holy hell on his head from behind."

"You should've said so." He reached out and laid a hand on my shoulder.

"I just did. Give me a break all right? It's been a rough day."

I pulled the pistol out of my bag and tucked it into the waist of my jeans; it hadn't proven quite as effective as I'd hoped, but I'll be damned if it didn't make me feel a little bit better. I clutched the false Libro to my chest as I got out of the car, groaning when my back went through a series of eye-rattling pops. Swift killed the engine and the lights as I made my way down the path.

"Don't get yourself killed before I get there," Swift called out.

"No promises." I waved and kept shambling down the path.

I could already see the shadow of the old shattered gate coming up ahead, creeping out of the darkness under the trees. The temperature dropped enough to make my nose run, and the fog started to creep in around the edges of everything, giving the wild orchard a haunted look.

The more paranoid part of me thought the horror movie vibe to be a grave portent, but the truth of the matter was that all autumn evenings in Hanford were cold, dark, foggy and miserable. I made my way through the crooked posts of the long gone gate and it felt like passing through an invisible wall of sludge, as if all around the area hung a pall of noxious, writhing energy.

Everything behind me faded away, I felt surrounded by a thick, cloying pressure. It was moist, humid and warm in defiance of the evening's chill. I caught a faint whiff of something rotten, and all the sounds of the freeway faded away, replaced by the sound of a distant wind howling through a tunnel.

I could feel forces at work, raising my hair up like static electricity; power moved here, lots of power. Ahead of me, I could see lights, tiny flickering jewels like stars hovering in the darkness. As I suspected, Henry must have begun the ritual to summon forth the Sleeper. I moved closer and began to hear a multitude of chattering whispers, a chorus of unnerving gibberish at the edge of my hearing. I stuck to the shadows, wanting to get as close as I could, see as much as I could.

Whatever else he was doing, the forces Henry tampered with were pulling the Other Side over, peeling back the sane, safe mask of reality.

The ruins of the farm materialized before me, along with a crowd of figures. My great-grandfather had been busy.

Kneeling in a circle around the foundations of the barn were six women, an assortment of ages, sizes, colors--whatever else the ritual called for, it didn't seem to be too picky in its victims so long as they were female. They were all stripped naked with their hands bound behind their backs and distant, glassy looks in their eyes. They were all swaying like grass in a gentle breeze. Above their heads were the shining jewels I'd seen as I approached, that now appeared to be small, pale balls of flickering blue and white flame.

At the center of it all stood Sarah, still dressed in her floral scrubs, with her eyes closed and arms raised up, reaching for the sky above her. Her mouth moved, issuing forth the torrent of whispers that filled the area. I hugged the tree line, inching closer, and between the ring of bound women I could see the true Libro Nihil lying at Sarah's feet with its pages fluttering in the alien wind that blew through clearing. But of Henry himself, I could see no sign.

Where the hell was he?

I would regret it, I knew it, but I took in a deep breath to steady myself and let my vision slide to the Other spectrum. The regret came immediately, as my brain struggled to comprehend the thing that floated in the air above the women.

A great, giant, black, pulsing thing that looked like a cloud of ink suspended in water extended tendrils of blackness out to wrap around the heads and necks of the women, and at its center leered the face of my great-grandfather himself. His mouth split in a rictus of a grin, black holes swirled where his eyes should be, but as sure as I could feel the wind on my skin I could feel his gaze boring straight into me.

I almost dropped my book when he spoke, his voice a soul-wrenching knife I felt inside of me as much as heard.

“Now we can begin,” Henry boomed.

18

Moment of truth time.

How sad would it be for the worst day in my entire, brief existence to end here? It would kind of make everything leading up to this moment pointless. No reason to wax existential about it, or to drag it out. Kind of figures, in a sad and funny kind of way that it would take the apocalypse for me to dig up what little courage I have.

I tried not to think about the fact that I was doing it all for free.

"Have you come to prostrate yourself before me?" Henry's voice rose out of the black cloud, roaring like a hurricane. "Will you join me in my glory?"

I grit my teeth and stepped out of the trees, entering the clearing. I hoped Swift had gotten into position nearby.

"Actually, yes." I held up my book, the false Libro Nihil. "And as a gesture of good faith, I've brought you a gift."

While Sarah continued her chanting, eyes locked shut in whatever mindfuck Henry trapped her in, and the women continued their swaying, the face of my great-grandfather creased in an ugly frown. A ripple went through the magic fluctuating in the air.

"Impossible," Henry growled.

I shrugged, taking a few more cautious steps forward and glancing furtively about as I did. The wispy tentacles that latched onto the women pulsed with ugly, dirty energy. I risked giving the lights floating over their heads a closer look and my heart skipped a beat.

It was their fragile living souls that hung over them, beating in time to the rhythm of their hearts.

"Impossible that you could have been duped?" It came

out shakier than I would have liked. "Flesh-Thing wasn't dead when I got to him, you know. Or should I say Knows-Secrets? He tricked you and gave me the real book, begged me to stop you with his dying breath. Check it out if you don't believe me."

I stopped outside of circle still holding up the book for him to see. The cloud around his face pulsed, throbbed, and he bared his teeth in a carnivorous grin.

"I'm impressed. You're not the simpering weakling I thought you were." Henry's voice washed over me with a graveyard stink. "You would damn humanity?"

"I decided it's better than the alternative." I somehow managed to match my gaze with the black holes where Henry's eyes should have been.

And then he laughed.

In the center of the circle the tendril wrapped around Sarah's neck disappeared in a puff and she hit the ground like a ragdoll, crumpling into a heap.

"Come take your place. Complete the ritual, awaken the Sleeper and bring forth this world's oblivion. The sacrifices are ready," Henry said. "I must thank you for delivering the last one to me."

The last what now?

The cloud stirred, from it a figure emerged and settled onto the ground. I didn't realize for a moment that I looked at the unconscious form of Hack, and then I gaped. With my sight shifted, I could see that the aura usually hanging around him like a thundercloud guttered like a dying candle. A tendril of smoky darkness extended from the cloud to wrap around his throat like the other sacrifices. His eyes closed, arms limp at his sides.

I wanted to say something, cry out, but I couldn't. He stood there, in the center of the circle next to where Sarah lay. It jarred me to see him, but I understood why Henry would have wanted him alive. Sacrificing Hack and releasing the energy contained within him would supercharge the ritual of the Libro Nihil and force the door between worlds wide open.

I made my way past the other sacrifices, trying not to look at their faces. If I messed up, I didn't need anything else weighing on my conscience. I kept my eyes away from Sarah, and the way she lay in the center of the circle without moving; instead, my eyes riveted to the spot where the true Libro Nihil sat with its pages fluttering. I only needed a second to make a grab for it, to disrupt the spell that Henry had already used Sarah to begin. I was also at ground zero for when he realized what was happening, which was convenient, and would be the first victim of his wrath when he realized I tricked him.

There was no easy way to do this. I could only hope Swift waited somewhere nearby waiting for his opening.

I held my false book out in front of me, lying flat and open across both my palms. I could feel Henry's attention on me, watching everything I did. I went through the motions of beginning a ritual, focusing my mind and drawing on the energy coalescing in the field. The air around me inside the circle shimmered, the scar that Abel Grannok left upon reality appearing like a ghostly ribbon suspended in the air.

And then I dropped the book.

"Fool!" Henry howled. "What are you doing?"

Hack and the other sacrifices stirred, the tentacles around their throats tightened. I ground my teeth and made my move, swept up the true Libro Nihil and pulled the pistol from the waist of my jeans with my other hand, raising it over my head, aiming for dead center of the cloud where Henry's face hovered.

"Swift, now!" I shouted, pulling the trigger, and the gun roared as it belched forth a torrent of fire.

A lot of things happened all at the same time.

The world exploded into a calamity of warring darkness and light. I couldn't process it all, but I did have the stupendous luck of standing smack dab in the middle of all the festivities.

It started with my great-grandfather screaming, a noise like the earth tearing itself apart, followed by a roughly humanoid shaped streak of white light slamming into the cloud. I got blown clear of the ritual circle by the tremendous force of the collision and thankfully had enough presence of mind to clutch onto the Libro Nihil for dear life when I went sailing through the air.

And then I proceeded to black out.

Consciousness came back piece by piece. It started with hearing, something like the sound of the ocean roaring in my ears and someone yelling my name over and over.

My body came next with a sudden awareness of all the pains I collected during the day flaring up all together while something shook me. Vision came last with my eyes opening to see everything in monochrome, and a hazy shape in front of me, the outline of a person.

"Tommy, god damn you get knocked out a lot!" Hack shouted.

He resolved by inches along with the rest of the world. Color started seeping in, and I saw his eyes were an ordinary, human shade of limpid brown. I think I tried to say something but my mouth didn't work right. There were hideous noises all around me of stone shattering, tortured metal screaming, and a furious, howling wind. Hack started yanking me to my feet and I noticed I still held the Libro Nihil, clutching it to my chest.

"Now ain't the time for spacing out," Hack shouted right next to my ear. "Your buddy Swift's working on getting himself killed."

My head swiveled on an uncertain neck in the direction of the riotous noise, and with my vision still tuned to the Other Side I got treated to a full-blown sensory assault.

I saw an angelic being of pure white fire, wings burning like the sun, Swift, hurtling down from the sky at the monstrosity that Henry had become, the seething black nightmare with his twisted grimace inside of its inky mass, dark as the void between worlds.

They crashed and slammed into each other, darkness and light smashing together in a whirling frenzy that my brain screamed to stop looking.

I could make out underneath all that chaos the still shapes of the sacrifices along with Sarah in the middle of it. They all lay still, the jewels of their souls shining dully above them. I turned to Hack and stared at him dumbly.

"We're all going to die."

"Shut your damn fool mouth with that talk." Hack glared, brow knitting together. "I taught you better than that. It ain't over yet."

He turned to watch the fight and I gasped at how crooked he had become, bent almost where once he stood strong and burned with power.

He appeared again as he did when I found him in the Bastille, a tired old man, and my mind whirled at the ramifications of that.

I didn't have time to worry about that.

He was right; of course he was right. What would I do? I didn't stand a chance against Henry in the shape I was in. I scratched at the cover of the Libro Nihil anxiously and for the briefest of moments gave strong consideration to running, putting as much distance between me and the whole terrible situation as I could. But some small part of me unfortunately decided to speak up and remind me I couldn't do that.

I would only be delaying an inevitable demise and damning the world to a horrible fate. Better to face it. I'd stopped Henry from using the stupid book to bring forth the Sleeper, and the end of the world with it, didn't mean I wouldn't get myself killed anyways.

The book?

I sighed and hung my head.

"Damn it," I muttered. "I am an unbelievable idiot."

"I could've told you that," Hack said.

I glared at him, then despite my body's every warning against it began edging towards where Henry and Swift battled. The Libro Nihil was the key, it always had been. It was the key to everything, and I felt like a complete ass for not having realized it sooner.

The true secret of the book, what made it an awesome relic of the supernatural, didn't lie in its power to punch holes through reality and conjure forth alien beings. What made it truly powerful was its supposed ability to compel creatures from the Other Side.

I let the flickering, barely there remnants of the energy inside me reach out to the book, and I could feel it, the roiling magic inside. It felt alive, a well of power that wanted to be used, that just needed someone to take the leash off and let it go to work. So much of power it scared me. The things a person could do with it were they so inclined; I could give life to miracles and nightmares.

Maybe later.

If I survived that long.

I flipped the book open, revealing its worn, yellowed pages covered in a scrawling script, filled with designs and formulas that made my eyes twitch as I looked at them. I laid a hand on it and brought everything I left inside me to focus on the strange magic that throbbed within the pages of the Libro Nihil. It was so much more than just a book. It reached out to me, latched onto me down to the last molecule and infused me with an almost overwhelming power.

My pain and worry and fear became small, far away, and I knew exactly what to do with complete certainty.

The thing that Henry had become surrounded Swift, enveloping the brightness of his form and smothering it.

I had no time to waste.

"Hey, Henry!" I shouted.

Henry's face swung around to look at me, still clutching. Shadowy tentacles stretched forth and raced at me intent on my destruction. Exactly as I hoped they would.

I raised the Libro Nihil and let loose the power inside it, the power to compel and control beings from the Other Side. Like the Sleeper, the well that Henry drew from. The book leapt from my hands and spread itself open mid-air, pages flipping and blurring, while the darkness surged forward. I prepared to fall back on my original plan of running like hell until a tremendous cry rose up from the black cloud.

The book sucked the tendrils into its pages like a vac-

uum. Henry's face twisted into a tortured grimace, screaming, howling and gnashing his teeth as the black cloud ripped away. I saw Swift hit the ground.

"This is not the end!" Henry howled.

"Yes, yes it is," I said finally, reaching up to take the book in my hands and feel the power of it as it worked. It was amazing.

It devoured the malignant, entropic power of the Sleeper into itself. Somewhere I could feel something happening; somewhere in a place that was not a place, far away and yet close enough to make my skin crawl. Something stirred, shifting, moaning in a fitful sleep.

As fast as it began, it all ended, Henry and the cloud gone, and the book slammed itself shut.

It left me shaking, body singing with adrenaline, still holding the Libro Nihil up over my head. It felt warm, and when I looked up I could see steam rising from its surface. I lowered it, staring at it, noticing not for the first time what a small thing it was. I must have zoned out; I jumped when Hack came up and put his hand on my shoulder.

"Well, I'll be damned boy," he said with something resembling pride in his voice, “you did it.”

For a second I stared at him, and then I smiled. And it hurt like hell.

“Yeah, I did, didn’t I?”

19

It took me a while to realize it was all over.

I stood in the middle of the clearing with Hack, still shaking from an absurd amount of adrenaline and the cold that rushed into the field when all the magic dispersed. Now that all the insanity was over with, night cloaked everything beneath the trees. The buzzing behind my eyes reminded me I still had my sight shifted across the spectrum and when I brought it back a weight lifted and I could breathe again. Everything was all so...

Normal.

"Little help here?" a voice called from nearby.

I turned to look and saw Swift lying amidst the would-be sacrifices. I made my way over and frowned at the mess of it all, the victims of Henry's madness. What would they think when they awoke?

In a kind universe, they wouldn't remember anything. Hack hobbled up behind me, spitting out a curse under his breath. Swift looked like he'd been through a meat grinder, and somewhere in the debacle his sunglasses got lost or destroyed. I extended a hand to him, and helped haul him off the ground.

"This is a god damn catastrophe," I said.

Swift nodded. "But we won."

Hack knelt over Sarah, checking her pulse and muttering something under his breath.

"What happened to him?" Swift leaned in and whispered.

I shrugged, I wish I knew. All his power, all the magic that sustained him was gone. But what with the world no longer in immediate peril there would be plenty of time for questions and sorting things out later. For the time being there was a lot of clean-up to worry about, like seven women whose families were no doubt quite worried over. I tucked the still warm Libro Nihil into my hoodie, and picked my way over to Hack.

"What do we do about them?" Hack looked up at me.

I shrugged and frowned when I realized I'd left my bag in Swift's car. "Call the cops and run like hell?"

"Going to be a whole lot of trouble when they wake up." Hack stood, wringing his hands.

It may be wrong, but I hoped the lot of them was too traumatized by the ordeal or too deep in a magical funk at the time to remember much of anything that had happened--at least enough to not give much of a statement to the police or newspaper.

That would suck.

"You two step back." Swift came forward. "I can take care of this part."

Hack gave him a wary look but complied, and we stepped back. Swift looked out over the women, his eyes flashed white, and power rose in the air, something different from the festering evil that so recently filled the clearing. It felt cool and brought with it a smell I could only describe as clean.

Swift spread his arms wide and spoke a single word and his voice rang out through the clearing like a bell, "Home."

The bodies faded away, no flash, no amazing burst of power or special effects. They disappeared, leaving behind no sign they'd been there at all.

"Malakhim," Hack said under his breath.

The hair on the back of my neck stood on end, and it took me a moment to realize I'd been holding my breath. I let it out in a gasp when it was all over and looked at Swift as he stood there with a peaceful look on his face. He turned to face me, and a small smile pulled up one corner of his mouth.

"Wow," I managed to say.

Hack shook his head and hugged himself, rubbing his arms at the cold. The temperature dropped pretty severely and I could see my breath, and we were officially standing around in an empty clearing in the middle of nowhere.

"Let's get the hell out of here." I shook my head and shuffled off.

We made our way back to where Swift had left his car. He cranked the heater up and I sighed at the simple pleasure of it. It'd been a strange, horrible, painful day and it was some kind of amazing how nice a little thing like being warm was. Hack and Swift were talking about something, but I found myself too busy admiring how soft the seats were to pay much attention.

"Thomas, wake up. You got to see this," Swift said, reaching over and shaking my shoulder.

Apparently, I'd gone and fallen asleep. I raised my head, rubbed at my eyes and peered out the window. We were at my house. The little glowing clock on the dashboard said it was almost midnight.

Parked out front was a small gathering of cars, low-riders and street racers. The boards were gone from all the windows and there was a soft, inviting orange light coming through them while a plume of smoke curled up from the chimney. The house was clean of all the blackened char from Henry and Hack's scuffle, and even the leaves from the giant old ash that blanketed the yard were raked into neat piles. For the first time in recent memory, the place looked decent.

It looked like an actual home.

"This does not bode well," I said as I dragged myself out

of the warm comfort of the car.

Hack and Swift followed behind me. The door was unlocked when I went to open it, and when I stepped inside I was greeted by the soft light of candles that had been placed on the various bookshelves and cabinets. All the white cloths were gone, along with every speck of dust and sign of the battle earlier.

My battered, muddy shoes squeaked on the freshly mopped floor. I could hear voices and laughter coming from the kitchen. I cast Hack and Swift a curious look, got a pair of shrugs, and made my way down the hall.

Rosa, Jesus, and some of his friends from the Gardens were there sitting around the table and eating what appeared to be a sprawling cooked meal of some kind. It smelled amazing, and I found myself salivating, my stomach growling. Jesus shot me a ridiculous grin, while Rosa sat quietly at the head of the table. The kitchen, like the rest of the house, had seen a thorough cleaning and candles were lit and strewn about everywhere.

"Hola brujo," Rosa said, not looking at me as she spoke, loading up a plate with beans and meat and rice. "Your power got shut off."

One of Jesus's friends got up and took his plate to the sink, so I dropped myself into the vacated chair. I drummed my fingers on the tabletop and looked around, taking it all in, letting my mind whirl. I grabbed a plate from the little stack on the table and began spooning large portions onto it. Hack and Swift hung back, waiting. I took a bite of the food, and another, and another. For a time, my entire world revolved around that plate of food. No one spoke. Everyone waited.

After I inhaled the last morsel of food off my plate, I sat back and let out a little sigh, folding my hands across my stomach and looked across the table at Rosa, who stared back.

"So, what the hell is this?" I asked.

"We couldn't stay at my sister's place, so I figured since you went and got my house wrecked me and my boy could stay here," Rosa said matter-of-factly. "It was disgusting though, so I cleaned it."

"Right. And I have no power?"

"When we got back, a city man came and shut it off. Said you ain't paid the bill in months," Jesus added helpfully.

Money grubbing bastards, every last one of them and

with Devlin gone they wouldn't be getting paid any time soon, either.

Hack settled himself into a chair when Jesus got up, and Swift wandered off. The rest of the gangsters followed, and as Jesus passed by he gave me a thumbs up and an odd wink. Weird kid.

Get my ass handed to me six ways to Sunday, save the world from an evil abstract cosmic entity and my insane, undead great-grandfather and what do I get for it? My home invaded.

I rose from the table and shuffled my way out of the kitchen.

"So, we can stay?" Rosa called out after me.

"Whatever." I waved.

I made my way to the stairs and trudged up to my room. It seemed to be the only place in the house that Rosa hadn't gone through. I entertained the thought of taking a shower and trying to wash off the day but decided it could wait till morning. Or next week, or whenever I woke up. I felt like I could drop into a coma.

The Libro Nihil was still in my hoodie, still warm as it nestled against me, and as I took it out and laid it on the nightstand beside my bed a sudden breeze went through the room.

"You're really going to keep it?" Swift asked from behind me.

I almost jumped out of my skin, my heart thudding in my chest like it was about to burst out of my ribs. I spun to face him.

"What the fuck is a matter with you?" I frowned and punched him in the chest.

He gave me a weird little smile and I noticed his eyes glowed, luminous points of white.

"Sorry. I was just wanted to say goodbye," Swift said, filling up the doorway. "It was a hell of a day. Definitely interesting. You did good, Thomas."

I frowned, dropping myself down onto the edge of my bed. I glanced at the Libro then back to Swift; he stood there watching me with his hands in his pockets.

"Thanks? I didn't die, but I guess that's the most I could really hope for." I shrugged. "And yeah, you're damn right I'm keeping the book. Better me than someone who would try to do something awful with it."

"Be careful. So, do you want to know the truth now?" Swift asked.

The truth.

The truth could be a scary thing, and sometimes a person was much better off without the burden of it. The truth about Swift? The scholar in me, the rabid junkie that craved information itched to know. But that little voice in me that kept popping up at the oddest times all day told me it might not be the best idea, that I might not like what I heard. It could open up a whole new can of worms and as of that exact moment I couldn't deal with anything else.

"No offense, Swift, but I think I don't actually give a damn anymore." I fell back onto my bed and let out a sigh.

"Smart man. Take care of yourself, Thomas. Don't do anything stupid," Swift's voice was quiet, like he was far away. "It's hard enough being your guardian angel."

I blinked and sat up, but I was by myself. Swift was gone.

I buried myself underneath a pile of blankets and pillows, trying to barricade myself away from the rest of the world. As much as I wanted to, sleep wouldn't come. A million questions roared through my head. What'd happened to Hack and where had his power gone? What was I going to do about Rosa and her son, and the small army of gangsters that followed them? How the hell was I going to get the electricity back on? Never mind the rest of my bills.

For a time my brain swirled and rattled, beating itself up with worries. I don't know what time it was when things began to finally fade, when sleep finally came to take me away. I remember one last thought, before I fell into the blissful and dreamless sleep of the exhausted.

What a fucking day.

Epilogue

“Feels like it’s been forever since I’ve done this...god, not since I was a little boy and my mom made me. Haha, can you believe--seriously--that my folks sent me to a psychologist, too? They thought maybe a growing boy with a peculiar ability might benefit from a more...clinical, perspective? I don’t know. I mean, obviously it didn’t help much, otherwise I wouldn’t be here talking to you, would I?”

“You going to order another drink, or what?”

I snorted, looking down at the half-melted ice cubes in an empty tumbler on the bar in front of me. God, I’d drank the whole damn thing already? I told Swift this was going to be a bad idea. What the hell was I thinking? Holy shit I'm drunk, my inner monologue's rambling to itself...

"Yeah give me another. Anyways, like I was saying, it's been forever since I've been to confession." Certain words and sounds were beginning to get a little difficult to make effectively.

The bar was suitably slow for a Tuesday, no, wait, Wednesday evening. Dear god who goes to a bar on a Wednesday? The bartender shook her head patiently, looking neither flustered nor like she gave any kind of particular damn as she worked magic behind the bar with glasses and bottles. She had the easy, practiced motions of a woman who'd been honing her craft for years; in the span of a few heartbeats, she was sliding a newly filled tumbler in front of me.

Her name was Ethel, and I found that hilarious.

"You don't say?" she didn't look up as she spoke, turning instead to wipe down the already clean bar top.

"I do say. Maybe that's my problem, you know?" I held the glass up to the light, staring into the brown liquid, watching the ice float. "Maybe I don't get shit off my chest enough, holding stuff in can be bad for you, right? I mean, fuck...I've seen some pretty messed up shit."

"Maybe it is better to just keep it inside," Ethel said, eyes turned towards the doors, focused on something a million miles away. Or she was trying to will someone to walk through them and save her.

"If you'd seen the bloated, undead remains of a primordially exalted anura-lich, would you keep that to yourself? You can't bottle that kind of thing up." The brown liquor burned, made me gasp a little and suck in air through clenched teeth.

"That's exactly the kind of thing you need to keep bottled up."

"And where the hell is Swift, anyways? Did he fall in the fucking toilet? Do angels of death even go to the bathroom? That guy's weird, let me tell you. You know I watched him punch a cerebraphage's face out the back of its skull before? And cerebraphage's have some big ass skulls, I mean, they're practically just a gigantic brain with legs anyways, am I right?"

I almost hacked up the last of the whiskey when I tried to take it all in one shot. A seasoned drinker I was not. I sputtered and rattled the ice cubes around in the glass, signaling Ethel for a refill. She never came. Blearily, I looked around the bar. Near as I could tell it was just me and the old TV set murmuring reruns of 'I Dream of Genie.' Ethel must have bailed.

"Excuse me? Ethel?" I called out, leaning over and peering behind the bar. No one. I looked around, "Anyone?"

I made to get up off the stool, wobbling on precarious legs. I clutched at the edge of the bar to steady myself, hoping the feeling of being on a storm-tossed ship would pass soon. Whoever invented alcohol was an asshole. What's the make the idiot who drinks it?

Footsteps sounded from nearby, distant through the haze of alcohol clouding my brain I could almost feel the telltale humming behind my eyes, something approaching…

"Ethel, thank god." I turned towards them.

And was flung into the air by an out of control mid-sized sedan, slammed full in the chest and tossed across the bar to go crashing into a sturdy old table and chairs.

"Not Ethel," the voice was like listening to rocks grind against each other deep underground, so low I felt it vibrating around the bones of my skull.

"No," I said, trying to pick myself up out of the wreckage, trying to bring the world into focus. "Definitely not Ethel."

The thing was so big the top of its head almost brushed the ceiling. I had no idea how it had gotten into the building, or how it'd managed to sneak up on me. Arms like tree trunks ended in knobby mallets, and even through the alcoholic blur, I could make out two narrow, bright orange eyes like coals, buried under a craggy brow.

"Grey-Man. Killed my brothers, prepare to die." The giant began its lumbering advance.

Brothers? What? Memories began swimming to the surface, images in fragments of two large, brutal figures. Ogres.

Ah, hell.

"So that must make you baby brother..." I didn't have time to put up any hope of defenses, so I did the next best thing and cowered in the colossal ogre's shadow and waited for death.

It let out a terrible battle cry, something like an old steam-engine's shrill, tortured howl that rattled my molars and shook the walls. I clenched my eyes and sphincter shut and tried to think brave thoughts. There was a terrific popping sound, and I got splattered with a thick, warm fluid that stank of burnt pork.

"What the fuck?"

My eyes blinked open in time to see the ogre crashing to its knees, nothing but a ragged, bloody stump north of its shoulders. Swift stood just behind it, trying to wipe greyish gore off his fist onto his jeans. More of the ogre's blood had splattered out onto the walls and ceilings, as well as onto me. It was gross.

"I can't leave you alone for five minutes, can I?" Swift came forward to assist me out of the rubble.

I looked around at the carnage. The ogre's body was already putrefying, disintegrating into a rank, and steaming puddle.

"Apparently not. Where the hell were you?"

"To call Rosa for a ride, promised her we wouldn't drink and drive, remember?"

I nodded numbly and let him begin escorting me out of the bar by the elbow. My head was starting to throb; saliva was flooding my mouth in the precursor to a violent round of throwing up. Should've known better than agreeing to go out drinking with Swift, should've stayed home. What kind of life is it where a guy can't even go out and get properly drunk without some supernatural, homicidal asshole coming to try and kill them?

My fucking life.

INTERMEZZO

Chasing Normal

I stood, shaking, trembling with little rolling waves that ran from head to toe, rattling my teeth and knocking the ends of my joints uncomfortably into each other.

It wasn't from the cold, though it was the ass end of winter and the season had decided to crank it up to eleven in one last blustering stretch of ridiculous cold and sopping rain. It had poured all night, and even now, with the sun rising feebly behind angry clouds the color of steel wool, there was a biting moisture in the air the seeped under my heavy old army coat and under my skin to settle in my blood and turn it into glacial sludge.

No, it wasn't the cold that made me shiver. And it wasn't the hip that had only just healed rolling in its socket, lancing pain up my side whenever I put too much weight on it and bringing unpleasant memories of undead feral swine.

The reason for my sudden palsy was much simpler, and much more terrifying, rooted in an anxiety that sunk its teeth into my grey matter. That most wretched and insidious of things; anxiety. I was deep within its grip.

I'd been standing in the nigh-empty parking lot for almost half an hour, struck dumb and motionless with anxiety on the blacktop that glistened with a sheen from last night's now frozen rain. The building before me was hideous, blocky and daunting, stucco walls slapped with a psychedelic shade of purple that my eyes reacted to violently.

There were stacks and vents on the rooftop, belching forth columns of smoke that carried a pungent, charnel reek with an undercurrent of stringent chemicals. And the worst thing of all, the unholy piece de resistance, was the cow.

The god damn, god awful cow.

The Mad Cow Burger was the single most popular fast

food establishment in town, and its mascot, its totem, was the Mad Cow his own demonic self. I stridently hoped whatever acid-dropping son of a bitch had designed that bovine beast was currently roasting on a spit in the darkest bowels of hell.

A leering, distorted caricature of a cow with gigantic, googly-eyes shot through with blown blood vessels and curling surrealist horns, decked out in a purple suit that matched the building's stucco, dancing between the huge plastic letters that proclaimed the company's name, while its mystifying udder undulated grotesquely in flashing neon.

What in the name of all the small gods and little fishes was I doing here? Where was a syphilitic therianthrope in need of disintegrating? Why wasn't the world choosing to end in a spontaneous, pointless conflagration?

Why, oh why, had they called back?

Weeks ago, after managing to snatch the world away from an impending cosmological apocalypse and escaping with most my sanity intact I had decided I couldn't take anymore. Finished, I couldn't put up with the bullshit of the Other Side any more. Too many close calls, too many lives lost for no good reason. Not the least of which being my primary source of income, Devlin Desmund -- rest his poor, inhuman soul.

Unfortunately, that meant I had to seek out alternative means to supplement my income, which meant job hunting. And for a guy like me, who'd spent his entire life cloistered away with magical tomes and bashed over the head with the hidden realities of the world that meant starting at the body. Yeah, sure, I could enchant a ball of lead to distort local gravity, or look up the stream of time to see the world's own memories, but none of those translated into relatable 'real world' skills. Hence, scraping the bottom of the barrel; fast-food, menial, tedious work guaranteed to chip away at my soul.

But damn it, I liked money. A lot.

After applying on-line, I never expected a call back. My application was pitiful, I had no previous work experience, and I didn't have a single business reference that classified as anything resembling human -- except for my roommate, who I'm pretty sure plotted daily for my gruesome demise.

But call back they did, and they wanted an interview. It made me simultaneously happy, and suspicious. What kind of company hires a thirty-something nobody with no work experience? People with absolutely no shits left to give, that's who. So I found a decent shirt, one with actual buttons and no questionable stains, and I arrived at the appointed place, at the appointed time.

So there I stood, a shivering mess, crippled with anxiety over a job interview. I'd never had a job interview in my life. I'd never had an actual job in my life. I couldn't even remember the last time I'd spoke to a person that wasn't wearing a human skin-mask.

Whatever. I'd saved the world, I'd fought unspeakable horrors from beyond the edges of creation, and I could totally kick a job interview's ass.

Maybe.

I ducked my chin to my chest, squared my shoulders and took a deep breath. I mentally harangued myself, and tried to focus on the quiet little glimmer of light inside myself, the little spark of power that was my connection to the wider universe and the flow of energy that underlay all creation. My happy place.

It helped, if only to still the shakes, and allow me to mechanically place one foot in front of the other. As soon as I had the massive glass doors of the joint open, though, I almost turned tail and ran not three feet inside.

I walked into a hot, humid wall of air so pungent with the smell of synthetic meat-funk it bored through my physical senses to assault me on a higher level. Something in the back of my head shriveled up and died. Bile rose. It was unpleasant.

How...how could people eat this shit?

The fluorescent lights were shockingly bright, too damn bright, casting a pall over all the tables and booths. The same psychedelic colors on the exterior of the building covered the insides, the nightmare purple paired with radioactive greens and nuclear oranges.

I didn't even work at the place yet, and already it was trying to filet my soul.

The only customers in the place were a loose collection of elderly gentlemen, speaking in hushed tones about simpler times and the proper methods of distributing fresh goose shit.

I swung my attention over to the counter that hung low on one wall like a black slug, its back lined with a row of hi-tech looking cash registers. Stationed at one of them was a bored looking young woman, maybe twenty, leaning a hip against the counter top and staring hypnotized at one of the light bays on the ceiling. I couldn't tell if it was some form of gratuitous, ironic humor, but her make-up was a perfect match to the color palette of the store.

I walked up and cleared my throat, trying to find my voice.

Her head swiveled down to face me, but she didn't quite look at me. I watched as her pupils dilated, then expanded, coming into focus.

"Welcome to the Mad Cow Burger," she said in the most bored, grating voice I'd ever heard. "Would you like to try a Dappled Pie?"

A what the fuck and what the hell? I blinked, a quick shudder racing through my body like an aftershock.

"What? No. Not even a little bit. I'm, uhh...here to see..." Oh dear god what was his name? "Del!"

I smacked a fist on the counter top. It was like pulling teeth from a polar bear barehanded, wringing that name out of my addled mind. I was proud of myself.

The service girl flinched and blinked owlishly at me, taking a great deal of mental strain to process everything. Finally, she nodded, and without a word made an abrupt about face and disappeared behind a wall that divided the counter and dining area from the mysterious kitchen in the back.

I shoved my hands into the pockets of my coat and shuffled back and forth while I waited. My eyes couldn't help but pass over the menu board and its display of supposed food stuffs. A gallery of maddening concoctions in colors no food was ever meant to be. But it was all incredibly cheap, shockingly so, and I began to understand the appeal Mad Cow held over people a little.

"You're Thomas Grey?"

I swung around to where the voice came from. Deep, raspy, tired as if every word were an effort that required infinite concentration and care.

The speaker was a prodigiously rotund man, not so much fat as just...very, very round. His skin was dusky, flesh hanging off him in drooping sacks, sealed up with a starched white shirt and cinched with a bright purple bow tie. He might have been in his sixties, but the fringe of short, frazzled hair and coal black eyes that appeared perpetually miffed made him look even older. He sized me up. Weighed me.

Judged me.

And from the subtle curl of his lip and nigh-bestial snort, he must have found me lacking.

Regardless, he shoved a meaty paw at me.

"I'm Del," he grunted. "You must be Thomas Grey."

I stared at his hand like an alien artifact. The gears in my skull box ground their teeth together. This was it. There was something I should do. Some quaint, time honored social interaction that normal humans performed countless times every day.

I slapped my hand across his palm, bumping my knuckles against his on the backswing.

"That'd be me," I said in a high-pitched nasal version of my own voice that sounded freakish even to my own ears.

Del's mouth sagged in a frown, dragging the jowls of his face down. He shook his head patiently and withdrew his hand, settling it and the other on his hips.

"All right then. Come with me." He turned and strode off

into the back of the store.

I followed, pulled along by his gravity, led into the secret world of Mad Cow that the common customer never sees. And never should see.

Baroque machinery, encrusted in layers of barnacle like grease hissed and popped, whirred and churned out symmetrical patties of meat, each station manned by a blank eyed worker in a drab black uniform. They moved as if they were machines themselves, their minds somewhere far away from the prevalent haze of smoke that hung about the kitchen.

Del led me all the way to the back, deep into the store's guts. I watched as he approached a simple white door set into the rear wall, a crooked placard holding a paper sign proclaiming 'MANAGER' in a dreadful choice of font. He twisted the knob and opened the door, stepping inside without a word, expecting me to follow in. Which I did.

"You can shut the door," he said.

I did, taking a quick glance around the office. It wasn't much of an office, as far as such things go. It more resembled a janitor's closet that someone had stuck a rickety metal desk into, a relic of a computer sitting atop it. Lining the walls were racks of shelves, piled high with an assortment of cleaning chemicals and utensils that gave the room an eye-burning odor.

Del settled himself into a little metal folding chair behind the desk, the thing letting out a pitiful groan as he did. There was a little manila folder sitting atop the desk that someone had written 'GREY, T.' on with black marker. Del jerked his head at another chair opposite his.

I set myself down in it, frowning, adjusting a few times and coming to the conclusion that the chair was purchased at a second-hand torture device emporium. There was no way to get comfortable.

"Why do you want to work at the Mad Cow, Thomas?" Del asked without looking at me, flipping the folder open and scanning its contents.

"Money. I like it," I blurted.

He grunted, arching an eyebrow without looking up at me, continuing to read.

"You're how old..?" He asked, with a hint of incredulity.

"Uhh thirty...four."

"And it says here you've never had a job?"

"No? Kind of?"

He mumbled something under his breath that I didn't quite catch, and then looked up at me.

"I'll be perfectly honest with you, Thomas," he said, folding his hands atop his desk. He shifted his bulk and continued, "I'm short-handed. I'm going to hire you--"

"Really?"

"But..."

"But?"

The man growled. Like a damn animal, he growled.

"But I don't expect you to last long. I don't know what it is, but there's...something about you. Something ain't right. You ain't right. You're a weirdo, I can tell. I slap you on service, let you take orders. Last damn thing I need is you killing yourself on the grill or some stupid thing. But soon as I find someone to replace you, or you make me regret being a kind and generous kind of guy, you're out. You hear me?" He narrowed his eyes after delivering his little speech.

I frowned.

I applauded the man's honesty, but I found myself kind of offended. I wasn't a violent guy, not really, but at that moment I wanted nothing more than to launch myself across the desk and channel unadulterated malice into his veins, pump his skull full of sickening pressure and liquefy his eyeballs. I could do it. I hated doing that kind of thing, but I could do it...

"Works for me, Del," I spoke through a smile and gritted teeth.

He took a moment, just watching me, and then nodded sharply as if making some kind of decision. He reached under his desk, pulled a bulging little paper bag out and tossed it across to me. I caught it and stared at him.

"Your uniform. Now get the hell out of my office. I got things to do." He'd already turned away from me to face his computer. "You start tomorrow, five o'clock bright and early."

The urge to kill rose at the mention of stupidly early o'clock. I sighed. Nodded, and got out of the monstrous little chair. As I left, I heard Del clacking away at his computer, and made my way back out of the miasma in the kitchen to the front of the store.

When I got outside, I took a deep breath of the air. It was cold, and sharp, and stung the back of my throat the way only valley winters can, but it was clean and glorious. I stood collecting myself, letting my little victory sink in. My first step on the path of normalcy. Mission accomplished. I had a job. A terrible, mindless, horrible fucking job that would end up being the final nudge that sent me over the brink and turned me into a vicious killing machine.

I should get a commendation for my gallant efforts at resisting the urge to become a violent psychotic.

"The shit I do to get paid," I mumbled and started the long walk home.

Night Terrors

I went slinking through the darkness...

I slink through...I slinked...slunk?

What a horrible word...

I went slow and careful through the inky darkness. Heel to toe, eyes closed, one hand out to brush fingertips light along the wall. I trusted to muscle memory and the mental map that a lifetime of habitual wandering had created.

A man's house was supposed to be his castle.

My house didn't even feel like my home, these days. Sure, I knew every nook and cranny, had wandered its hallways countless times, spent my entire life cloistered behind the security of its walls...but something had come to my ancestral stomping grounds.

Violated it. Corrupted it.

Twisted it and made it their own, claiming a bestial dominance that brooked no contest and made me a prisoner in my own home.

So I found myself shuffling about like a thief in the night, sneaking downstairs, mindful of each footfall so as not to make groan the old floors. My heart thundered around in my chest, bouncing off my ribs, the manic rhythm of it loud in my ears. If I got caught, if I got spotted sneaking around in the middle of the night...

No, it didn't bear thinking on.

My stomach growled as I made it to the foot of the stairs. I hadn't eaten all day - got caught up at working a slave shift in the salt mines - and by the time I'd gotten home, dinner was gone, and it was all my fault I'd missed it. I'd been too soul-weary to argue, and passed out in my work clothes. Reeking of salt and grease.

But vengeful need had driven me from oblivion, and I chose to embark on a perilous midnight adventure for sustenance. A budding ascendant master requires fuel, regardless of the evil machinations of inhuman wardens.

All was quiet. So far, so good. Not much further and I'd be in the clear. Safe and nestled in the sanctuary of the kitchen. I hazarded opening my eyes a slit, spectral forms coming out of the gloom like geometric ghosts. My old furniture, older than I was. Motes of dust drifted through the air and beyond the landing of the stairs a yawning black tunnel - the hall that would lead to the kitchen.

My journey was swift; I must have pleased whatever wee god looked down upon me. I made it into the kitchen, and instinctively snapped a hand out at the light switch on the wall, flooding the room with near-blinding light. I threw my hands up to guard my eyes, gasping.

Slowly, blinking, while tears welled up in my eyes, the room brought itself into focus. Shapes began resolving into familiar objects. The counter. The blessed fridge. The dining table. And hovering over the dining table, eyes baleful and bright with fury...

I screamed and turned to run. In my frantic haste, I lost all sense of direction and plowed face first into the wall behind me, bouncing off it and crashing in a heap on the scuffed linoleum.

I'd hit the wall solidly with my face; blood poured out of my nose, which in turn throbbed and beat jagged blows of pain into my skull in time with my heart beat. I groaned, staring up at the tiny little super nova's that exploded in front of my watering eyes. A shadow made its way over me, descending by inches, and a deep-seated, primal dread replaced the pain in my face.

"Just when I start thinking you can't possibly be any dumber, you go and prove me wrong, brujo," Rosa said from above me. Everything she said always had the hint of accusation behind it.

"What did I ever do to deserve this?" I moaned from the floor. I rose with a grimace, head swimming as I did, reaching a hand up to pinch my nose and block the waning flow of blood, wincing. I made it to my feet and turned to face the terrifying woman, "You're not human."

Something of a feral smile crooked her lips, violence

flashing behind her eyes, "More than you." She settled herself into one of the chairs at the dining table.

I gave her and the table a wide berth, edging towards the counters that lined the kitchen. I felt around at the drawers below them, snagging one open and rustling out a dishtowel. I shoved it up against my face to soak up the blood. I wasn't hungry anymore. I'd swallowed too much blood. I was already getting a bit nauseous.

"What're you doing hiding in the dark, anyways?" My voice came out muffled and nasal.

Rosa turned to look at me. The grave look was gone, replaced by a tired facade that deepened the wrinkles at the corners of her eyes that made her look more like just an exhausted lady than a monstrous tyrant. "Nightmares, brujo."

I nodded. "Yeah, I get those, too."

Something in her eyes hardened, narrowing at me. When she spoke, it was slowly, "How do you do it? How do you... the whole world's fucked up." She folded her arms over her chest, holding herself. She looked almost fragile.

I knew better. Rosa was anything but fragile. She was a

hard woman. Fierce, even. Raising a kid all on her own in the middle of a disputed war zone. Working herself half to death to provide for him. And then finding out that the world is even scarier than she could've ever imagined. Finding out that monsters are real; she'd seen the human kind, gang bangers and criminals that care nothing for human life - the real monsters just piled more on.

But she was also the same woman who, when face to face with a gargantuan beast threatening her child, flew into attack. She exploded like retribution incarnate, like a terrible deity of frightful destruction.

She went flying across a room and smashed a fucking footstool across an ogre's face. It was pretty amazing.

"The world's always been fucked up, Rosa." I settled back against the counter, daubing the rag at my nose. "It's just...now you know how well and truly fucked it actually is. I mean, yeah, sure, now you know there are extradimensional horrors lurking at the edges of reality, and the bogeyman is real, but...shit. We still got to eat, right? Still got bills to pay. Lives to live. Try to live."

She mulled my words over.

“Why do you do it?” She asked.

“Do what?”

“All the stupid shit you do. I ain’t known you too long, but I’ve already seen you damn near die more times than I can count. Why?”

Fantastic question, actually. For a guy who says he wants nothing more than to be left alone to his own devices, I got into a massively disproportionate amount of trouble. I was too damn young to feel so damn old. Life threatening encounters with things that should not be took their toll on a guy. But, and there was always a but...

“Someone’s got to, I guess.” I tossed the bloody rag onto the counter. Blinking, I looked back to Rosa, “Someone’s got to throw a wrench in the works. We humans, by and large, are an ignorant lot. And we’re happy to be that way, too, more’s the pity. But, guys like me, who know the uncomfortable truth; I guess there’s a kind of obligation there.”

Rosa quirked a brow but remained quiet.

“With the knowledge I have, and the weird shit that I can do, I could by rights be a really fucked up person - if I felt like it.”

I pushed away from the counter and went to the table. I sat down across from Rosa and looked at her levelly, "Or I can do my best to protect humanity's ignorant self, and try not to die in the process. I guess it is pretty stupid, when you think about it."

She let out a sigh and closed her eyes. It was like watching her decompress. She sort of sank, her shoulders sagged, and her chin drooped. She shook her head and lifted it, as if just waking up. When she looked at me, her face was smooth, relaxed, her eyes clear of anger or tension. "Want something to eat?"

I blinked owlishly. "Yeah, yeah that would be cool."

She rose from the chair and made her way to the fridge, calling back over her shoulder as she did, "Good. Now shut up. Your talking's giving me a headache."

Kind Words

"You know what your problem is?" Hack growled, punctuating each word with a blow from a hammer as he drove pickets into the dirt.

That's a hell of a question to ask a guy. And we'd been doing so well, too. This is what I get for volunteering to help a geriatric old bastard fence in his hopeless garden so he doesn't have a labor-induced stroke. We had been working in an almost amicable silence for the last half hour, the season finally relinquishing its hold on winter's chill only to make way for an early bout of unreasonable heat.

There weren't 'seasons' so much in the valley, at least not a full cycle of them like some places found themselves with. Just a never ending battle between the extremes of summer and winter. Good times.

"Eh, let me think. The universe is trying to kill me; I'm roommates with a half-senile, moribund redneck and a hostile cleaning lady. Not to mention a job that is killing my soul by inches. Oh, yeah, and my best friend is a fucking angel of death." I ticked off each statement without looking up, piling pickets in a row to for planting in the ground.

Hack made an ugly rumbling noise deep in his chest, then I heard him hock up half a lung and spit. A thick, black and yellow wad of mucus landed inches from my feet.

I blinked. Turning slowly to look up at him, he had crossed his arms over his grizzled chest, hammer dangling loose from one hand. He was staring at me with his eyes squinted, an almost malevolent look to them under the shadows of his craggy, bushy brows.

"No, Tommy," he said flatly. "Your problem is you're an asshole."

"Who the hell shit in your corn flakes?"

Beneath the wiry confines of his beard, his mouth cracked into a smile that revealed as many gaps as teeth. The last few months had been hard on him, ever since losing his connection to magic. Whatever mysterious ailment it was that was wasting him away, it was beginning to get obvious. He was no longer stocky and built like an old, gnarled oak. He'd lost a lot of weight, skin developing a texture akin to old paper and sprouting liver spots in curious patterns. And while his beard was as bristly and glorious as ever, his hair had thinned to the point that he'd begun taking a razor to his skull.

"Don't tell me it ain't true, boy. You run around, acting like you don't give half a shit. Hiding up in your room, sticking your nose in books all damn day. Acting like the fucking world's got it out for you. Pinky little baby Jesus, I swear, you got your head so far up your own ass you don't know which way you're going." He shook his head, smile widening. He thought he was hilarious.

I bit the inside of my mouth so hard it began to bleed, biting off the vitriolic retort I really, truly, wanted to spew. What the hell was he getting at? Seriously.

"Is there a point to this abuse, old man?" I asked, speaking through clenched teeth.

He nodded, stooping to gather up another picket and settle its end in the dirt. He laid the head of the hammer on it, eyeballing it, sizing it up.

"The point, you big girl, is you're an asshole. You don't have a damn clue what you're actually capable of, because you're too god damned scared to do what you really want to do." He raised the hammer and brought it down. A single, solid blow and the picket drove itself six inches into the ground.

"What I really want to do, right now, is knock your rickety old block off you cantankerous fart."

Hack barked out a laugh, a real whopper. Complete with knee slapping. It devolved quickly, turning into a fit of wracking, full-bodied coughs. It only lasted a moment but left him gasping in shaky breaths of air, and he looked up at me with a lop-sided grin and wiped tears from his eyes.

"Well then do it, if you can find your balls," he said and stood up straight, planting his feet.

My hands clenched into fists. I did my best to shoot eye-daggers at him. The power inside me, feeding off my rising anger at his provocation, whirled dangerously in the back of my brain. The pressure of it built, pushing at the insides of my skull. It would be the easiest thing in the world to cut-loose and just...

Do something I'd regret. A lot.

I squeezed my eyes shut, squeezing my hands so tight my nails dug into my palms. A took in a deep breath, held it, and when I released it I let it take the swelling, violent energy with it. When I opened my eyes, Hack was watching me with an unreadable expression on his face. The empty space in my brain where the power had been filled up with static, like air rushing into a vacuum. It made my ears ring for a second.

"You know what makes me different from the Others? From the fucking monsters and bastards, and the psychotic mages that have no issue with raping creation to get whatever they want?" My voice came out flat, tired.

Hack's only response was to crook a single brow up.

"I know better. Magic's not a fucking weapon; it's not wish fulfillment. There are consequences, most the time horrible ones -- I know that real fucking well. You taught me that, remember?" When I let my hands unclench, my knuckles popped.

Hack nodded and stooped to pick up another picket.

"You're right," he said. "Don't you ever go forgetting that, either. No matter what kind of madness the world tosses you, whatever choices you have to make, don't you ever forget that. Now go get the damn hose. Squash ain't going to water itself."

I frowned. Damn old man and his damn lessons. I muttered a half-assed string of expletives under my breath and turned to go retrieve the hose from the side of the house. As I walked off, I could hear Hack grumbling to himself.

"What kind of damn fool kid goes and tries to magic up a money tree, anyways? You really are an asshole, Tommy..."

Stardust

There are secret things and secret places in this world that infringe upon the boundaries that separate it from the Other Side and what lies beyond. Sometimes it's a place of recurrent atrocity that touches upon some aspect of one of the many underworlds, sometimes it's an object that resonates with the vibrations of an elemental plane. And sometimes a piece of the Other Side finds itself over here, ripped away by unseen, alien hands and placed for alien reasons in our world. I've come to expect these occurrences in small-towns, which in my not inconsiderable experience are magnets for strange events and happenings. I couldn't be entirely sure why; maybe it has something to do with the sheer, banal concentration of humanity in larger cities that keeps the Other away. But I've seen enough in the valley to know if I were a smarter person I would've moved the hell out a long time ago.

But I'm not a smart person, and I doubt I could leave the valley even if I wanted to. Not with the way things have been going around Hanford lately. Small town strangeness keeps getting stranger. Ever since the Sleeper debacle and my acquiring of the Libro Nihil it's been a madhouse, probably not least of which because Devlin Desmund was no longer around to keep the peace between the disparate factions of Others. His death left a power vacuum that Swift and I had been scrambling to fill. Even Uncle Satan had marshaled his people into a misfit militia, working around the clock to keep the less savory Others from boiling over and causing too much havoc. It had worked so far, but we couldn't keep it up forever. At one point I thought I'd hold down a real job, like normal people do but I should've known that was doomed from the start--being anything but normal myself it was probably a bit foolish to even try.

So it was that I found myself with a rare moment to relax after settling a territory dispute between a raucous spirit of decay and a local grocer when Rosa burst into my room, shattering my peace. In my exhaustion, I'd forgotten to arm my defensive wards and charms against entry, and now it seemed I would pay the price.

"Brujo!" She hollered as she did most things. "Get your lazy ass up and get moving, muy malo out there; what do you think you're doing?"

I blinked, slowly, two or three times and thought perhaps if I wished real hard I would disappear, or maybe she would. But it didn't happen. Some slinger of cosmic forces I was. Instead she advanced and looked like she was about to take a swing at me. I might have flinched, maybe raised my arms to protect my head, but the blow never came.

"Dammit, brujo," she said and her voice was quieter, layered with bone-deep exhaustion I couldn't help but relate to. "There's something crazy going on at work, I need you to take a look at it." I heard her feet shuffle back, and quieter than before she said, "Por favor."

There was a part of me that almost asked her to repeat that last bit, but it was an often times suicidal part and I shoved it back down in its place. Pushing myself up and out of my chair, wincing at the series of creaks and protestations my body let out, I reached over to flick on my desk lamp.

"Something happened at the hotel?" I began putting things in my pockets, my phone, a couple stumps of chalk, and a lighter. Anything to not look at Rosa, standing there in her housekeeper's uniform, at the dark circles around her eyes that were still fierce and bright, defiant, despite the pall of fear that hung around her. Something had rattled her, something pretty bad. I'd seen her take swings at inhuman monstrosities literally twice her size without hesitating.

"Yeah, something. You got to come see, it's..." I turned to look at her as her words trailed off, to see her struggling with what to say next. When she continued her tone was clipped, careful, "One of the girls is missing."

"Huh?"

Rosa scowled. "There's something in one of the rooms. Something weird has been going on in there all week. Maricella, the other housekeeper, she went in there tonight…she never came back out."

"The room ate her?"

"Ay dios, brujo I don't know, that's why I came to you."

She really looked like she was about to hit me now, out of sheer frustration. My brain hummed. Rosa worked at a real scum dive, a cheap hotel on the east side of town by the freeway that was frequented by criminals and junkies, often used as a meeting and hunting ground for predators of the human and inhuman varieties. The manager, a sick bastard I'd had the displeasure of meeting once, took cash only and held his silence about the goings on at his establishment, and unless there was gunfire and explosions the cops typically steered clear. My first thought was that an Other had gotten sloppy, picked off one of the housekeepers, and would need aggressive persuading to vacate the premises. But, really, who knew?

"Did you check the room?" I asked.

"Not on your life, no." She crossed herself and shook her head. "There's something evil in there, brujo. I can feel it. It ain't right."

For all that she was a vanilla mortal, Rosa had sharp instincts, and had been exposed to the Other Side on more than one occasion. She knew what she was talking about.

"I'll check it out. You'll have to give me a ride, Swift's out on business. I'll meet you down at the car, okay?"

She nodded and left the room without another word, leaving me alone with my thoughts for a moment. No rest for the wicked, as the saying went. The town kept getting stranger, and the strange kept getting more dangerous. Something was coming, a storm, a catastrophe; I could only hope to be ready for it when it hit. Before leaving, I opened up the top right drawer of my desk and looked inside with a sigh at the lone object within.

A tiny, pocket bible sized book with a plain, black leather cover and worn out spine, faded with age.

The Libro Nihil.

"All right, you bastard," I said as I reached down for the book. "Time to get to work."

•••

The Stardust Motel sat in a dirt lot at the end of a road heading east out of Hanford, and was the last stop in that direction before a wayward traveler found themselves on the north-south bound freeway. Two stories of dilapidated mess, the whole thing looked like it was minutes away from collapsing under its own ponderous weight. Built sometime in the fifties with that era's taste for angles and curves, and a great big sign in sputtering neon blue hung from its façade, once upon a time it might have been a classy joint. But once upon a time had passed, and the decades since its last renovation were long gone. Now its bright, hopeful blues and whites had faded and become sickly yellows and greys that spoke volumes of the decay that permeated the place, of the rot that lingered around it. There was a curious range of cars in its lot, beaters and pickups and a conspicuous Mercedes parked next to a florist's delivery van. Rosa and I sat across the street in her little hybrid, watching the place. It was near to sundown and nothing moved, everyone holed away in their rooms for a night of god only knew what.

"That's Senor Wyzant's car, the Mercedes he bought right after he said he couldn't afford to give us raises." Rosa's scowl was incendiary. She would have made an amazing mage, had her cosmic cards been aligned right.

"Well I'm probably going to need you to distract him while I go figure out whatever it is that's going on," I said and gave myself a final pat down to make sure I had everything I thought I would need. "Which room did you say it was?"

"Two-oh-nine, brujo," she said and flicked a hand towards the building. "Second floor, by the vending machine."

"Oh, awesome." I frowned. "Hey, uh, do you have a dollar?"

"Que?"

"I'm hungry, all right? Didn't eat before we left."

She muttered a string of elaborate curses and profanities in Spanish but produced a crumpled bill from a wad of cash in her purse. Not wanting to test my luck, I got out of the car and made a wide circle around the building, approaching it slowly, giving Rosa time to get out and make her way to the lobby at the front and the esteemed Mister Wyzant's office.

I got that old, familiar itch as soon as my feet touched the gravel of the parking lot. The gnawing of tiny worms behind my eyes. The quiet squeal deep within my grey matter. Something very Other, and very wrong, was afoot. Moving in a shambling crouch and sticking to the deepening shadows, I hid myself behind a bush growing along the side of the building. In a room nearby someone was blasting death metal, the monstrous din muffled by distance and stucco, but it made a disconcerting backdrop to the vibes I was picking up from the building. With a blink and a held breath, I slid my vision across the Other Side, shivering at the sensation of a slender blade working its way between the hemispheres of my brain.

As I opened my eyes and let go my breath I looked up, at the second story, and began considering setting cleansing fire to the building as a reasonable option. Whatever it was in room 209, it was of a magnitude of wrong that I had rarely witnessed outside abstract cosmic forces. And that did not bode well.

That did not bode well at all.

Rays of what could not quite be described as light slid and rolled down the balcony walkway of the second story, greasy fractals that were hard to track, hard to look at for more than a few seconds without sending my primitive monkey brain into a gibbering panic. The door itself was a whorl of chaos, bulging out through the dimensions, something massive pressing up against the barrier between worlds, something stretching the fabric dangerously taut.

"What the hell?" I hissed and shut my vision down, getting back to normal. My eyes burned, and there was an alkaline taste in my mouth like I'd been sucking on a battery. "This isn't cool. Not cool at all."

I focused on the thunderous staccato coming from the nearby room and detached myself from the shadows behind the bush, sparing a glance towards the lobby in time to see Rosa talking to a gaunt, pallid man whose bald pate gleamed with sweat under the cheap fluorescents despite the cool of the coming evening. Satisfied she would keep him distracted I made my way to the stairs at the end of the building that led up to the second story. Every step was a quiet agony, as if walking into a searing wind that blistered my mind and tugged at my soul. A mage's connection with the forces of creation is as much a burden as a blessing; while I can alter the flow of reality and bend it to my whim; those same forces alter me as well. And right now the whole 'burn it down and consequences be damned' idea was starting to sound better and better. A magical salvo of cosmic fire from across the street would be taxing, but I had a hard time believing anyone would really miss the Stardust when it was all over.

By the time I got to the landing at the second story I was out of breath, clutching at the guide rail of the stairs with a white-knuckled fist. Room 209 all but called out to me like a siren, monstrous, luring me to an unspeakable demise--if in some bizarre Homeric adaptation sirens were hotel rooms?

But for a change, simple human biology came to the rescue; my stomach growled and clenched, and I doubled over in a vicious hunger spasm.

"Okay," I muttered and fished the crumpled dollar Rosa had given me out of my pocket. "Okay, maybe I should eat before opening the doorway to unknown horrors most foul."

There was no telling how long any of the snacks in the vending machine had been there and I didn't have the time or inclination to care. I had a bad habit of neglecting basic necessities, like eating, and later paying the price for it. Puny flesh bag. Fighting for my life against hideous otherworldly forces--not to mention slinging magic--was taxing, and hunger made a person weak, made them slow. I jammed the bill into the slot in the front of the machine and punched a couple keys corresponding to a large candy bar. Sustenance and sugar, cherish the simple pleasures.

The vending machine clanked and rattled, parts thunking and moving around in a series of spasmodic motions entirely too convoluted and slow for delivering a candy bar to a starving man. At last, the blessed thing dropped and I shoved my hand through the swinging gate at the bottom to catch my prize. I had the wrapper off and half the chocolate concoction stuffed in my mouth in the space between heartbeats, and was choking down the rest in the three steps it took to get from the vending machine to stand at last in front of the faded, battered door to Room 209.

My head pounded, my eyes watered. I beat my chest with a fist and gasped. Protip: don't inhale food.

"Better," I wheezed out.

But still my head throbbed and I became aware of warmth in my pocket. The Libro Nihil was waking up, reacting to whatever waited inside. Soon the little book felt like a hot coal pressed against my thigh--it was eager. That wasn't good.

"Fine, let's do this." I stepped forward, reaching for the

doorknob, but the door popped open as I did and swung inward on groaning hinges. That was never good, either. “All right, then.”

And like an idiot, I stepped inside.

•••

Whatever it was I had been expecting when I passed over the threshold, a spacious, well-lit room with three-piece furniture set including a large bed that took up most the space and large flat screen TV mounted on the wall was not it. From the outside I figured I would be walking into a festering den of vermin, maybe even get real lucky and find a corpse putrefying in the corner with towers of refuse and unidentifiable stains on the walls and carpet, that kind of thing, not tasteful, pastoral prints on the walls and the lingering smell of lavender.

The whole space was lit by a pale light from a single fixture overhead, muting the shadows in the room and softening the edges of everything, giving it all a--dare I say it--otherworldly ambience.

It didn’t make sense. A symphony of tiny dental drills whined inside my skull and there was a palpable weight, a pressure to the air, a presence I couldn’t identify. I pulled out the Libro Nihil and ran my thumb along its spine. It responded with a tingle not unlike static electricity, the book vibrating in my hand, and I couldn't shake the feeling that it was responding to whatever it was that was in the room with me.

Any minute the trap would spring and I would be fighting for my life and sanity against who knew what kind of abomination, I was sure of it. I began scanning the room, taking it all in; I didn't dare shift across the spectrums to view the Other Side, I didn't think I was prepared, let alone equipped for what I might see.

"What the hell are you doing, Thomas?" My voice came out sounding hollow and falling away.

I kept looking around, shuffling about with slow half-steps like I was walking through a minefield. All the while I scanned the walls, the TV, the bed. The cover on the bed was a pristine white, pure, a bizarre absence of all color that made it seem brighter than the light above. It was so white that the tiny black box on it appeared like a void in my vision.

Black box?

I had been looking around for minutes, had swept my

gaze over the bed a number of times, and I was certain there had been no fist-sized black box sitting serenely atop the covers of the bed a second ago. I stared at it, blinked, stared more and it was still there as if that was where it had been all along.

"Oh fuck you," I said to it.

The box, of course, said nothing.

It was small enough to sit comfortably in the palm of my hand, and its sides were perfectly smooth, perfectly flat and reflected no light. It was so dark it almost seemed to be swallowing the light, and from the way it pressed into the mattress it must have weighed far more than it should for its size. The more I looked at it the more the inside of my skull whined and the backs of my eyes felt like ants were gnawing at them. It was definitely the culprit, whatever it was.

The Libro Nihil was shaking like a living thing in my hand and somehow managing to pull at me, like it was trying to get to the box.

"None of that now," I growled and shoved the book back into my pocket. I barely understood the Libro Nihil, it had only been in my possession for a few months, but what I knew of it was that it was an item of monstrous, alien power and a sentience dwelt within it I couldn't fathom. It was also the vessel the essences of an untold number of Others it had devoured in the long centuries of its existence.

If the Libro wanted the box--whatever the hell the box was--it probably wasn't a good idea to let it have it.

"No way around it, then," I said to the room. I had a bad habit of talking to empty spaces. "Let's see what you're all about."

I shifted across the spectrums like pulling off a bandage, quick and with my teeth clenched together.

It was the sudden and overwhelming vertigo I was least prepared for, and for a few breathless moments I found myself fighting to stay on my feet as the world spun around me like a mad carnival ride. The room was gone, and from the looks of it, so was everything else.

Space surrounded me on all sides, the kind that was filled with stars. Except that it wasn't. Filled, that is. There was endless darkness broken here and there by a fitful spot of light, like a pinprick in a vast black tapestry behind which a candle guttered feebly. Without thinking of the how or whys--those always came later, in my experience--I gasped as I spun about, wheeling free of gravity. It was the most elaborate, not to mention expansive, glamour I'd ever witnessed let alone experienced. Far, far off in the distance above me something moved and I craned my head to see a roiling disk of not-light, like I had seen in the hallway when I first arrived at the Stardust. It was spinning at a glacial pace, and at its heart lay a spot of darkness deeper than the void in which it spun, so massive I could feel its dread weight and gravity pulling at me. Gas and vapor and dust, the detritus of planets and other bodies hurtled into that cosmic maw.

A black hole, I was looking at a black hole.

"Beautiful, isn't it?" The voice came from right behind me, breath warm against the back of my neck.

I flailed and spun around, trying not to jump out of my skin, trying to raise my defenses and finding that my power felt as far away as the stars that flickered in the distance. It took some doing but I managed to stabilize myself but I finally turned around. For a glamour it felt entirely too much like I was hanging in space.

"It's no glamour, Thomas," the woman in front of me

said. “You know that, you’re only now pushing past the fear to accept it.”

She was tall, a head and then some taller than myself, and she wore a trailing gown woven of a material the same color as the darkness that surrounded us, the same color as her eyes. Her skin was porcelain white, and it made her eyes seem as deep as the black hole that spun in its ravenous dance. She wasn’t beautiful, not by any stretch, but there was something about the sharp cast of her features, fullness of her pale lips and cheeks, that couldn’t be described as anything but alluring. The hair that framed her head and face and neck was black as well, and I began to pick up on a certain theme.

“That’s right.” Something like the ghost of a smile curled the corners of her mouth.

“Get out of my head.” I scowled and found my hands clenching into fists. “Please.”

One sable brow arched and she nodded. A pressure I hadn’t even been completely aware of lifted, and I found myself able to move more freely, and when I reached for it felt my power as well like a comfortable warmth inside my chest. It wasn’t something I always consciously thought of, my gift, in the way that you never think of your eyes until you're searching for something you can't find. With a courage born in no small part from a growing anger, I scrutinize the woman, picking through the layers of reality and magic and gasp as the truth dawns at last: there is no woman, there never was. I've been staring at the black hole the entire time. Or, I should say, what I thought was only a black hole. The woman was there for my convenience, something for my feeble, limited mind to process without unhinging.

And the not-woman nods.

She, it, whatever exudes a silent but implacable power, like the seas or the sun or the motion of the planets themselves, a natural, undeniable force and that power is hungry and will not be denied. It is the hunger that devours stars, that slows the dance of galaxies to a crawl and that waits at the end of all things. It is entropy and decay, and I know it; I carry an infinitesimal fragment of it within the Libro Nihil.

"You're the goddamn Sleeper." I consider calling for my own power, unleashing the Libro Nihil. And then realize it would be less than pointless. I was only there because the thing that was the Sleeper wanted me to be. In the same moment, my stuttering brain lets loose a thought not borne of fear or anger. “But you’re not asleep.”

Another incline of the head and those black, bottomless eyes stare into mine.

“Not completely, no,” the Sleeper says. “This piece of me is awake while the rest lies dreaming.”

“What do you want?”

“Isn’t it obvious, Thomas? I want to make you a deal.”

I should have just burned down the whole damn hotel.

•••

For what felt like half an eternity the thing that was not a woman stared at me, and I stared back at it. The bottomless eyes and inhuman visage, not to mention the monstrous alien intellect behind the whole façade, made it impossible to tell what it might be thinking.

I had better things to be doing.

Probably.

“You realize how ridiculous you sound, right?” I asked.

The Sleeper’s puppet frowned and cocked its head to the

side that reminded me of a confused dog...

"Seriously," I continued. I couldn't afford to slow down. "What the hell could I possibly have to offer you that you couldn't just take? I thought you Entropics were the all-powerful cosmic abstract types?"

There you go, Thomas. Piss off the alien god of ruin. The puppet face shifted, frown deepening. It twitched. Its mask was beginning to slip.

Never underestimate the power of simple, human audacity.

"Unless, of course," I steamrolled forward, pulling the Libro Nihil out of my pocket, "you can't just take it. Can you?"

Something stirred beneath the puppet's perfect, porcelain skin, rippling and coiling below the surface of its face. I tried not to stare.

"You haven't even heard what I'm offering," the puppet spoke, slowly, obviously restraining itself. "I could make you a god."

I raised a hand, the one holding the Libro Nihil, and shook my head. "That didn't work out so well for old Henry did it? Thanks but no, if you want whatever bit of yourself is trapped in this book, you're welcome to try and take it."

And I waited.

The Sleeper's puppet fairly shook, and whatever it was that lurked beneath its mask pressed closer to the surface, writhing like a snake pushing to burst free of old skin. As I watched, a hairline crack began to form under one abyssal eye, and fingers of not-light seeped out.

Odds were I was going to get myself killed. But I had to test a theory.

"I will make you know fear, worm. I will make you know pain," the puppet hissed, hands clenching open and shut at its sides. "You will give me what is mine."

"Fear? I'm not scared of you." I shook my head and even barked a short laugh. "Have you even met my roommate? No, sleepy-pants. I'm not giving you anything, and I'm starting to believe you can't take it. Actually, I'm willing to bet you're just about powerless to do anything at all right now."

Cue agony.

The puppet's skin exploded as lances of not-light burst

through it in every direction. There was a roar of sound like a million waves crashing onto a million shores. Something like a colossal serpent made of shadows and light filled my vision before all I could make out was a wall of static that consumed my entire being, and every atom of my body felt like it was on fire.

Through the roar of sound came a voice that threatened to split my skull apart.

"I could consume you, Thomas Grey. Worm. I could scatter you upon the void and annihilate everything you hold dear." The Sleeper boomed inside my head.

I wanted to scream. I think I was screaming, already, and it had consumed my whole body.

Time ceased to exist. There was only the pain and the scream I had become.

Pain was something I had become intimately familiar with over the years, after a lifetime and career of sticking my nose in inhuman affairs; it had become something I was used to experiencing. And even though the Sleeper was introducing me to a whole new level there was a part of my mind that managed to remain functioning through it all, and I felt a familiar vibration humming up my arm and raised my hand.

The Libro Nihil leapt from my outstretched hand and flipped open, pages fluttering rapidly. There was a thunderclap and then I wasn't alone in my screaming. The tidal roar shifted pitch, became a howl, and I felt myself drop to my feet on what felt a lot like solid ground. Through a fog of pain and a cacophony of inhuman screaming in my skull, vision began to return, and I saw multiple scenes layered atop each other as the spectrums of reality clashed.

Deep within the void of space I saw a monstrous singularity roaring in cosmic fury.

Inside a dingy hotel room in a town in the middle of nowhere I saw a smooth, black box from which a hideous serpent of shadows and light writhed.

"You will live to regret this, worm," the Sleeper's voice boomed inside my skull. "You will know despair. I will let you live long enough to see all you know obliterated, before I devour you."

"Oh fuck you," I snarled and stepped forward, holding the Libro Nihil out like a pistol. It was like walking into a hurricane.

The hotel room, the whole world, shook and the serpent of shadow and light that was the Sleeper howled as ephemeral, ghostly tendrils lashed out of the Libro Nihil and enveloped it before snapping back and taking it inside the book.

There was a final, horrific cacophony of sound, the death throes of the cosmos, and then everything went dark.

•••

I came to with a gasp, lurching upright and scrabbling at the dark while my heart pounded against the inside of my chest like a terrified animal.

A dim, red light illuminated the area around me and I looked around in confusion. I wasn't in the hotel room, or floating in space. The red light came from the display of a small clock radio--my clock radio. I blinked and shook my head, ground the heels of my hands into my eyes.

"What?" My mouth was parched and when I took my hands away from my eyes, I took a moment to breathe and calm down, to collect myself. "What?"

I was in my room, my quiet little den of comfortable chaos, in my chair in front of my desk. There was a terrible crick in my neck, and my back was stiff. A second and third look around the room confirmed it for sure: it was definitely my room, definitely my home.

"A dream?" I mumbled to the darkness. "For fuck's sake."

Visions of monstrous serpents and dead-eyed porcelain women lurked in my mind, and a voice promising doom still echoed in my mind. Something moved at the corner of my vision and a dry, rasping sound came from nearby. I shuddered and turned to see the Libro Nihil in the middle of my desk, laying open, pages fluttering from a breeze that was coming in from the window behind my desk. I frowned and squinted at it.

"I don't think I like you," I said to the little book and reached out to pick it up and my fingertips tingled when I touched it, strange but pleasant. "Yeah...no more reading tonight."

I opened the top right drawer of the desk and tossed it inside. It landed with a heavy thump, heavier and louder than such a small thing should make but I was too tired, too disturbed to give it thought, and I closed the drawer and rose from my chair.

"Books are evil," I mumbled and shuffled my way across the warzone of my bedroom to collapse in a heap on my bed.

And when darkness came to take me away, it brought no dreams or nightmares with it, only peaceful oblivion.

No Holidays

I never asked my parents for anything for Christmas. Not once. I mean, they got me stuff, the tree was usually piled high every year with gifts wrapped in exotic, shimmering paper from wild, foreign lands. One year I got a Vision Stone from Mu that let me actually see my dreams right in front of me, played out in a surreal, holographic projection. I still have the thing, somewhere.

But I never made a list, and I never asked them for anything.

How could I when the next time they went out the door

could be the last time I ever saw them? Seeing them come back home was worth more than every Christmas morning. Grandpa would always tell me not to worry, that they would come back, that they always came back, that when the two of them were together there was nothing that could stop them.

And looking at them together, my mom and my dad, I believed it. The fierce, raw power that flowed between them, born of their love, could defy Oblivion - and had, on more than one occasion.

But then they would go, and the fear would creep in. Grandpa would take me fishing, or we would go up north to watch the stone-people work the underground gardens. He would show me ancient, secret magics that had been passed down to him by his father that he passed on to my father and would someday be handed down to me. But always there was the fear.

Weeks would go by, and sometimes months, but Grandpa was always right. Mom and dad always came back and there would be hugs and presents and stories, and for a little while the house was bright and warm and full of life.

Until something happened and they had to go away

again.

Until something happened and they didn't come back.

Grandpa woke me up in the middle of the night and promised me everything would be fine, that he was going to bring my parents back home.

And two days later Hack showed up at the door, the sapphire light in his eyes dim.

"I'm sorry, boy," he said.

Christmas was taken off the calendar after that.

Made in the USA
San Bernardino, CA
20 June 2017